THE PASS

A Smart Jocks Novel

REBECCA JENSHAK

Rebecca Jenshak
www.rebeccajenshak.com
Cover Design by Jena Brignola
Cover Photo by Wander Aguiar
Editing by Ellie McLove at My Brother's Editor

The characters and events in this book are fictitious. Names, characters,
places, and plots are a product of the author's imagination. Any similarity to
real persons, living or dead, is coincidental and not intended by the author.

❀ Created with Vellum

Chapter One

TANNER

Two years ago

"I feel like Cinderella." My buddy, Datson, spins in a circle, his arms held out to his sides and head tipped back in wonder, in the entryway of The White House, Valley University's unofficial basketball house, best party spot on campus, and our new digs.

I snort and drop my bag on the tile floor. "It's a little hard to picture you in a dress, dude."

"I guess that makes me your fairy godmother then." Joel skips down the stairs to greet us. His dad, the university president, owns the house, so he basically is our fairy godmother. This place is a palace. "Welcome, guys."

"This is so dope," Datson says, still taking it all in like he's never been here before.

There are only four bedrooms at The White House and being asked to move in is an honor. With the new school year, two of the previous guys graduated, opening up two spots. Joel lives here, as does our other teammate Nathan.

"Wes and Zeke's rooms are all cleaned out for you guys. We're having a party tonight, so get settled in and then let's celebrate." Joel claps me on the shoulder and then heads off toward the kitchen.

Datson and I go upstairs, stopping briefly to stare inside the half-sized basketball court that we're now going to be able to use anytime we want. It's just one of the perks of living here. There's also a theater room and a back yard with a huge pool and lots of space that's perfect for parties.

"Sure beats dorm living." Datson takes a step down the hall. "Which room do you want?"

"I don't care, man. I don't plan on spending a lot of time in it when I can be outside in that pool."

I let him pick and then walk into the other one. It isn't a lot bigger than my dorm room was, but it's a hell of a lot nicer. The walls are white and smell like they've been painted recently. A mural of the Valley U Roadrunner mascot is above the bed and there's a stack of bedding folded neatly on the end of the mattress. A desk and chair round out the furniture in the room.

After putting away my stuff and taking a shower, I don a pair of swim trunks and a T-shirt and head outside. It's early, but a few guys from the team are already out back chilling by the pool. The White House is the unofficial hangout even for the guys that live in the dorm or off campus.

"Incoming." Datson tosses me a beer as I take a lounge chair next to him.

I catch it like I'm cradling a football, pop the top, and take a long drink of the icy-cold beer. "Fuck, this is the life."

"I may never go to class again."

Nathan, the team's resident partier and now one of my new roommates is sitting on the hot cement in jeans rolled up so he can dangle his feet in the water, cigarette in hand. "I tried that. Turns out you aren't allowed to live here if you flunk out." He smirks so I think he's kidding, but you never know with Nathan. I wouldn't put anything past him.

"Yo, Nate." Datson holds up a beer and when Nathan turns, he throws it to him. Nathan catches it but then tosses it back. "No thanks, man, I'm good right now."

"Pacing yourself?" I ask. "That's new." Nathan's usually the first person with a drink in his hand and the last person to stop.

"It's going to be a long night. I suggest you do the same. The back-to-school party every year is insane and now you can't just leave to get away from it."

"Sounds rad to me," Datson says as Nathan stands and pulls out his phone, ignoring us. "Why would I ever want to leave an awesome party?"

"No clue." I hold up my beer. "Cheers to a long night."

An hour later, I'm three deep when I notice the party has really started to bump. All around shirts are coming off—that's always a good sign fun is being had—and people are jumping into the pool. That's exactly where I am, watching the patio where Valley U students continue to pour out.

Datson named himself party host and is jumping around chatting people up, offering cups, and acting like he's lived here for years instead of two hours.

Several of my teammates are in the pool with me shooting the Nerf basketball into the hoop set up on one end, but I don't have any interest in playing.

I spot Nathan near the edge of the pool. He's got a cute blonde hanging on him, but he doesn't seem to be enjoying her company. She's got fun written all over her which I would have guessed is his type. He tips his head to me in the universal sign for, *go ahead, she's all yours*, and I start toward them, but not before she throws her arms around an unsuspecting Nathan and brings him down into the water fully clothed.

"Oh shit." I bust up laughing, as does everyone else that witnessed it.

She's giggling when they resurface, but he is not. Nathan climbs out, jeans and shirt sticking to his body, mouth in a hard, straight line. I haven't quite figured out what his problem is until I see him walking toward a chick from our communications class. She's a transfer and hot. Hot enough to ditch a good time apparently.

I reach them as he and the communications chick, Chloe, are saying hello. I jut my chin in greeting to her and then slap a hand on Nathan's wet shoulder. "Dude, that was hilarious. You should have seen your face when she pulled you in."

He responds, I'm almost positive, but I lose the ability to hear. I scan the group of girls with Chloe and my gaze gets stuck on a tall blonde with big brown eyes that render me stupid. She's wearing a neon pink dress that hugs her athletic frame. She's staring at me too, although not quite so blatantly. Her gaze flits to me and then darts away. A shy smile tugs at her lips.

I know I'm gawking but I'm having a hard time doing anything about it until Nathan interrupts my thoughts by elbowing me in the ribs. "Shaw, can you lend Maureen some dry clothes?"

"Definitely," I say without thinking and before I realize Maureen is the girl that took him down in the pool and not the one I'm currently eye fucking. Reluctantly, I give my attention to Maureen who bats her eyelashes at me as she wrings out her dripping wet hair. I wrap an arm around her shoulders while not taking my eyes off Chloe's friend. "Right, yeah, come with me."

As quickly as I can without being rude, I get Maureen some dry clothes and a fresh drink, then head back outside. Chloe and Nathan are nowhere in sight, but the friend in the neon dress is easy to spot. As I'm making my way toward her, she turns away from her group of friends as if she could feel me coming.

"Hey," I say. "I didn't get a chance to introduce myself back there. I'm—"

"Tanner Shaw," she finishes for me. "I mean, I know. We're in communications class together. I sit in the row in front of you to the left."

"You're in our class too? The one with Chloe and Nathan?" I could have sworn Chloe was sitting by herself in there, and this girl isn't someone you miss.

She smirks. "Yep."

Damn, how did I miss her?

"Sorry, I must have been actually listening to the professor. First week of classes habit."

She laughs. "I'm Sydney."

"Well, Sydney, I promise I won't overlook you again."

Damn, way to sound like a creep. But seriously, I feel like someone just told me Bigfoot exists and I've been walking by him my whole life without noticing.

"Do you want to hang out?" I motion with my head to the pool.

"I'm here with some of my teammates. I don't want to ditch them." The group of girls behind her sneak glances at us as they arrange patio chairs so they can sit together.

"All right, well, got room for one more?"

"You want to hang out with us?"

"I want to hang out with you," I correct her.

She grins. "Absolutely."

We're just getting situated and Sydney is introducing me to her teammates when Nathan and Chloe rejoin us looking cozy. Definitely something going on there.

"Aren't they cute together?" Sydney says to her roommate. Emily, I think she said her name was.

Emily sighs. "Chloe's been at Valley U for less than a month and already has a boyfriend. I've been here a year and nothing."

Boyfriend? Well, damn, I didn't think Nathan had it in him, but it explains his newfound disinterest in getting shit-faced and partying with randoms.

Girlfriends aren't normally my thing. The commitment doesn't freak me out, I'm just not interested in the drama that often seems to follow. Playing two sports means I don't ever have an off-season. Getting up early, working out, long practices—it's a lifestyle for me.

The girls play twenty questions with the happy couple while I focus my attention on Sydney.

"What year are you?"

"Sophomore."

"Same." I think back, really peeved that I haven't run into her before. How is that even possible? "Have you been at parties here before?"

Maybe she doesn't party much or had a boyfriend last year?

"I have and a few at the baseball house, too."

"You know I play baseball?"

"Yes, Tanner, I know you play baseball and basketball. I know that you were the third highest scorer on the basketball team last season and your saves on the baseball team are on track to be the best of any closer the school's ever seen."

My brows lift and hide under the hair hanging onto my forehead. *Damn.*

"I like sports."

"That is hot."

She smiles and arches a brow.

"Not that you like sports, though that's super cool. It's hot that you know my stats."

"I know a lot of people's stats."

"Let's not talk about them."

Chuckling and shaking her head, Sydney smiles at me. "You're as cocky as they say."

"You're way hotter than they say."

She looks like she's going to ask so I add, "No one's said, but damn if I'm not real pissed that they haven't."

She's grinning and still shaking her head at me.

"Do you want another drink?" I need to stand, move around. I'm so amped up talking to this girl.

"Can I see the gym inside?" she asks and then bites her lip.

"The basketball court?"

She nods enthusiastically.

That isn't a request I imagined getting from a chick tonight, but far be it for me to deny this girl anything. "Sure."

With our drinks, we walk inside and weave through the party. When she nearly loses me in the crowd, she reaches out and grabs my elbow. Heat races up my arm at her touch. I slow long enough for her to get a good grip. Her skin is soft, but her hold is strong.

The guys have always kept the court locked during parties, so I've never been in here myself while people are over. I unlock it and hold the door open for her to enter first.

"Wow." She walks in, tilting her head up and then turning to take it all in.

I follow, staring at her. The gym is cool, but Sydney is a fucking wet dream.

"This is amazing, Tanner. If I had a place to practice volleyball in my house, I'd never leave it." Her gaze finally lands on me and her face is lit up with such excitement it stirs something inside of me.

She continues her exploration as she walks toward the rack of basketballs. Reaching out, she lets her fingertips graze the tops of the balls.

"Do you want to play?"

Glancing over her shoulder, she asks, "Basketball?"

"Sure, why not?"

She picks up one of the balls and turns it over, running her palms along the leather. It's as if she's someone who played a long time ago and is getting a feel for it again, reacquainting herself with an old friend.

She steps out of her heels and pads over to the top of the key. I didn't bother turning the light on when we walked in, so it's dark, only the skylights giving us enough illumination to see. She checks it to me, and I send it back, intrigued and anxious to see if she can play.

With a hesitant start, she dribbles twice with her right hand before switching to her left. I'm too far away to steal it without moving so she takes her time dribbling in place before she takes a step to the basket.

I let her come to me. When she's less than an arm's length away, I place a hand at her hip. It's a small amount of contact that I do almost instinctively when I'm defending, putting pressure on the offense and letting them know I'm not going to allow them to go where they want, but my fingers tingle as she presses back into me, pushing me toward the basket.

Sydney is fairly tall. I'm over six feet and the top of her head, even slightly bent over with the ball, comes up to my chin. Her frame is slender but strong and she doesn't seem intimidated despite how impressive she thinks my stats are.

Oh, and she definitely played ball at some point in her life. She naturally turns, angling her body to keep the basketball farther away. Her blonde hair brushes against my bare chest. She smells like cotton candy—sweet and addictive.

"What position did you play? Guard?" I guess.

She backs me up to the foul line where I refuse to give up any more ground quite so easily. And I'm not going to lie, her body pressed into mine is foreplay I didn't even know I was missing. I've never dated a chick who played basketball, or that had any real athletic ability. Now I wonder if I've missed out on a bunch more things because I've never been this excited about the idea of kissing someone.

"Forward." Sydney plants her left foot between mine and turns so she can get a half step in front of me and pulls up for a shot. I could block it, but I don't. I watch as the ball rolls off her fingertips and sails through the air, and the look of excited anticipation while she waits to see if it's going in. And I keep on staring, not really caring if it goes in or not, as she raises her arms in victory.

When I was a little girl, the boys loved having me on their team. Kick ball, tag, soccer, it didn't matter. I wasn't afraid to get dirty and play hard. I didn't even know that made me somehow different from a lot of other girls until I started school.

I showed up for kindergarten in my pretty new dresses and shiny shoes and went home with scrapes on my knees and dirt from head to toe. After the first week and five ruined dresses, my mother suggested we go shopping for more practical clothes I could play in. That's not what I wanted, though. I liked my pretty dresses and I liked running through the playground wearing them.

There was always something magical to me about being the girliest girl but still being a badass, even if that's not how I would have described it at five. Fifteen years later and it still feels pretty magical to see the admiration in Tanner Shaw's eyes as I drill a jumper from behind the free throw line.

"Bet you can't do it again." He rebounds the ball and walks

it to me. His light brown hair and blue eyes look darker in the shadowed room.

When I reach out to take it, he holds on, the tips of our fingers touching. A fluttering in my stomach reminds me I had a purpose for the evening and unfortunately it isn't getting friendly with Tanner Shaw. My competitive side really wants to make him eat his words.

"I should get back to my teammates."

"You sure?" It doesn't seem like he's asking me because he doesn't want to leave, but because he doesn't believe I really want to.

And I don't. Basketball may not be my first love, but I miss it. I gave it up in high school to focus on volleyball. While Tanner makes it look easy juggling more than one sport, it's almost impossible for anyone to do it and be successful at either, let alone both.

"I'm sure. Tonight is supposed to be about team building, getting Chloe and the new freshmen into the fold."

He nods slowly. "I get that."

After racking the ball, he leads me out of the gym and back downstairs. We get fresh drinks and I think he's going to leave me, but instead he follows me back to the group.

"Hey," Chloe says, looking happy I've returned. She's the real reason I need to be out here. Chloe is a senior transfer who came to Valley after a scandal at her last university. I've avoided reading any of the headlines myself, but from the gossip, I know her parents paid to get her in. There are also rumors that they made sure she played, but her performance speaks for itself—she's one of the best collegiate beach volley-ball players in the country.

The girls on the team, mainly our captain Bri, are dead set on shunning her, but I like Chloe. She's rooming with Emily,

Bri, and me, and so far everything I've seen from her has been genuine. She hasn't given me any reason to dislike her, and she works harder at practice than anyone. I appreciate a good work ethic.

So, tonight is about letting the rest of the team get a glimpse of the real Chloe. Tanner Shaw wasn't on the agenda, but I can't say I'm disappointed I finally got to meet him.

When I saw him in our shared communications class, I thought that was going to be my opening, but he hasn't so much as glanced my way until tonight. Dresses for the win again.

"Be right back," Tanner whispers in my ear. His warm breath sends a new host of goose bumps racing over my skin.

I take a seat, half-listening to the conversation around me as I watch Tanner navigate around the party. He's stopped every couple of steps by someone calling to him—guys and girls. The hot pink trunks he's wearing make me smile. They've got little alligators all over them. Not a lot of guys would dare try to pull off hot pink, but he does and pulling them off he is. I love that he doesn't take himself too seriously.

His body is lean and muscular. He has a great back and his ass... a real work of art. He leans over, giving me a really good view of said artwork, and I sigh. Emily shoots me a weird look.

I attempt to make my staring a little less obvious as I continue to watch Tanner grab his T-shirt from a chair and pull it on. He glances back at me and a slow smile pulls at his lips.

As he walks through the party, across the large back yard, I can't take my eyes off him. And his gaze only diverts from me when someone speaks to him. I've never had this sort of instant chemistry with someone. Or instant as soon as he noticed me.

I mean, I've been into the guy for more than a year, ever since I stepped onto the Valley U campus and first saw him. He'd been at The Hideout, a local restaurant and bar, with a group of basketball players. That was the first time, and since then, it feels like he's everywhere I turn. My body is highly tuned to Tanner Shaw.

When he reaches our group, he goes around my chair and drops into the small space behind me. His shoulder rests against my back and I lean into him.

"What'd I miss?"

"Oh, uh…" I can't very well admit I haven't been listening. "Not much. Nice trunks, by the way."

He looks down. "You like? My sister picked these out."

Tanner is better at following the conversation than I am. Yet somehow he still makes me feel special. A brush of his fingertips against mine, a whispered comment where only I can hear, the constant contact of his body against mine. There's nothing overtly sexual about any of his touches, but I am so keyed up that I barely notice the hours fly by.

Much sooner than I'd like, the girls are fading. Chloe yawns and it sets off a domino effect.

"We should probably go. Sydney and I have an eight o'clock class in the morning," Chloe says.

"Me too," Em agrees and stretches.

I groan. I know they're right, it's time to go, but I'm afraid that after tonight, things will go back to how they were before where Tanner doesn't notice me.

We all stand and start walking toward the house.

"Hey, wait," Tanner says before I'm through the door.

I fall back and let the rest of my teammates go ahead.

"Can I get your number?"

Hesitating, I wonder what the right move is. Am I being

too eager if I give him my number? The last guy I jumped into things too quickly with stopped calling after I slept with him on our second date.

But do I really want to blow my chance with Tanner?

"How about you give me your number?" I suggest.

He smirks but takes my phone as I hold it out to him. He punches in his number and hands it back, holding on when I try to pull it away. "You're going to call, right?"

"Sydney!" Emily shouts ahead of me.

"I have to go." He lets go of my phone and I take a step. "I'll see you in class."

"Are you almost ready?" Emily asks, sticking her head into my room. Her brows furrow. "Did you change?"

"The other shirt was wrinkled." Not untrue but normally I couldn't care less about what I look like for classes. Is it a coincidence that the first time Tanner noticed me was when I was in a dress and not my everyday clothes of shorts and a T-shirt? I'm guessing not.

It's been two days since he gave me his number and so far I've just stared at it a lot trying to decide what to do with it. Having the power, as it turns out, is a lot of responsibility.

"Well, let's go. We have five minutes to get across campus."

I grab my backpack and swipe a tube of lip gloss off my desk. Good enough. My first class of the day is speech. We're doing three-minute introduction speeches this week, but Emily and I have already gone, so I take my seat and zone out thinking about Tanner while others take their turn.

Fifty minutes has never gone by so slowly. I'm the first to

the door when the professor dismisses us. Emily stretches her long legs to catch me. "What is up with you?"

"Nothing."

Her smile starts small and widens before she erupts in laughter. "You're legit running to get to class to see Shaw."

I slow my pace. "Am not."

This makes her laugh harder. It's no secret that I have a thing for Tanner Shaw, but I thought I'd played it cool enough that my friends couldn't see just how crazy he makes me.

"You are. Slow down. Let him get to class first for a change. That way you can walk in front of him." She exaggerates her steps, swaying her hips from side to side and then flipping her blonde curls.

I give her a death stare and she nudges me with her elbow. "What happened with you two the other night?"

"Nothing really. He showed me the gym, we played basketball, and then you were there for the rest."

"That's it?" She seems disappointed. Me too, girl. Me too.

"He asked for my number."

Her eyes widen. "Did he text?"

"I didn't give it to him, but I got his."

"Wait." She stops. "He asked for your number and you told him no? Are you crazy? You've been completely hung up on this guy for over a year."

Okay, so obviously I haven't played it cool.

"If I'd given him my number and he hadn't called I'd be disappointed or worse, sitting around waiting and hoping he'd call. This way I have the power." Power I now realize that I don't want.

"I guess. So, what did you say when you texted him?"

"I haven't yet."

"Oh." She blows out a breath. "Why not? He isn't the kind of guy you play hard to get with."

We fall back into step heading to our communications class. I have a sinking feeling in my stomach that I've screwed this up. Tanner can get any girl he wants. Excited, eager girls who don't hesitate when he asks for their number.

My stomach is queasy when we push into the auditorium and I spot Tanner in his usual seat. I stare at my feet as Emily and I pass by, but I can feel the moment his gaze lands on me. I can't help it. I look up and meet his stare. He smiles and a little bit of the uneasiness fades.

Professor Sanchez starts just as I sit. I steal another quick glance at Tanner, his eyes still on me, and then pull out my notebook and my phone.

I start out jotting down notes for the group project that was assigned last class, but five minutes in, I'm scrolling through my phone and looking for Tanner in my contacts. When I find him, I click on his number and create a new message.

Me: Hey, it's Sydney.

Power reassigned.

Setting my phone down, I don't dare look back to see if he's checking his phone. Maybe he doesn't even bring it to—

My heart skips when a new message lights up the screen.

Tanner: Hey! Forty-eight hours... I thought you were never going to text.

Me: More like thirty-three hours.

Tanner: Thirty-three too many. What are you up to tonight? Want to hang out?

It feels like we're volleying back and forth and I just want him to keep the ball on his side of the net. I'm not usually one to back down or shy away from a good back and forth, but Tanner makes me feel all spun up and out of sorts. I'm too into him and I really hate that.

Me: Free after practice. Sounds fun.

Tanner: Shit, I forgot we have a team dinner tonight. Maybe this weekend?

Me: Maybe.

I'm hanging in the theater room, texting around to see what's going on tonight, when Nathan pops in. "Hey, what are you doing later?"

"I don't know. Football guys are having a party, a few people are going to the baseball house, Datson and Benny are at the Prickly Pear."

"Come with me to The Hideout."

"Who's there?"

"Chloe and her roommates."

"Sydney?"

Nathan pauses. "Is she the one with the long, blonde hair?"

I scoff. The one with the long, blonde hair? That's the best he can do to describe her? "She's the *super* hot one. Long legs, big brown eyes, heart-shaped face, killer smile..."

He gives me a blank stare.

With an eye roll, I say, "Yeah, dude, she's the one with the long, blonde hair."

"Cool. I'm going to find Chloe. Pick us up at Freddy dorm

in thirty minutes?" He lifts his arms and taps the archway and then leaves.

I'm on my feet and jogging up the stairs to get ready before he's out the front door. After taking a quick shower, I flip through my closet to find something to wear.

Joel stops in the open doorway of my room. "Hey, everything good? I haven't had a chance to talk with you since you moved in."

"Yeah, it's great. I really appreciate it." Not only is living in The White House cheaper than the dorms, it's across the street from our practice and game facility. It's all upside.

"Going out tonight?" he questions.

"Yeah, Nathan and I are going to The Hideout. You want to come?"

"Nah, I'm heading over to Katrina's. Have fun."

I figured as much. He's almost never here, I've come to realize. He stays at his girlfriend's place most nights.

I go back to finding the right T-shirt and jeans combination. As I'm pulling on a white shirt, my phone pings. I'm only a little disappointed when it's Tara instead of Sydney.

Tara: Hey! Are you still coming home next weekend for my game?

Me: Planning on it.

Tara: Yay! Best big brother EVER.

Chuckling, I toss my phone on the bed. I can almost see Tara's face and hear her voice through her texts. Only fifteen months younger than me, Tara and I are close. Our parents raised us like twins, putting us in all the same activities. If one of us wanted to play a sport or learn an instrument, the other one had to, too.

Those six months she thought she wanted to be a ballerina were rough. I totally showed up those little girls with my kickass pirouette though. And her interests did have some benefits. For example, I was voted the best dressed guy in my senior class thanks to Tara picking out my entire wardrobe. Sadly, I'm still hopeless without her help.

I button my jeans and walk to my bed and pick up the phone again.

Me: Are T-shirt and jeans okay for a sort-of date?

Tara: Define sort-of date? Where are you going? Is it just the two of you?

Me: Going to a bar and then maybe back to my place to hang out and no, there will be other people with us.

Tara: That doesn't sound anything like a date.

Me: I said "sort-of".

Tara: Boys are dumb.

Me: Noted. Now help me, please.

Tara: Send me a picture, full-length.

Me: Calling you so this is less painful.

I press the button to FaceTime her and prop up my phone on my desk. Stepping back so she can see my entire outfit, I feel a little ridiculous when her face appears on the screen.

"Where are you?" I ask by way of greeting. It's noisy and people are walking around behind her.

"I'm at the lake house for the weekend."

"Oh, nice. Did you take the boat out?"

"Focus, brother."

"Right." I hold my arms out from my sides. "Well?"

Her lip curls up and she tilts her head side to side. "It's okay."

My shoulders slump and I groan.

"I'm sorry, T, but it's so boring. The white T-shirt is played out."

"It's classic," I argue.

"Corinne," Tara calls. "Tell Tanner his outfit sucks."

My sister's long-time friend, Corinne, appears next to her. "Hey Tanner."

"Hey, Corinne. Help a guy out? I look okay, right?" Again, I hold my arms out. Corinne always takes my side. Ganging up on my sister is our favorite pastime. But the look on her face as she scrutinizes my outfit is not encouraging.

"It's not bad." She smiles hesitantly.

"Great, I was hoping she'd take one look at me and say, 'Eh, not bad'."

Tara and Corinne roll their eyes at me in perfect synchronization.

I tip my head back and stare up at the boring white ceiling. Fuck, *I'm* a boring white ceiling.

"Can you two help me or what? I have five minutes before I have to leave to pick her up."

"God, he's such a drama queen," my sister says to her friend who nods in agreement. "Picking her up is a good move though, props for that."

I smile tightly. No reason to tell them I wasn't actually the one who decided that part.

"Do you have anything that isn't black, white, or gray?" Corinne asks.

I go to my closet and pull out the first three shirts that meet that criteria and bring them closer for their inspection.

"Oooh," they say in unison and then turn to one another.

That sounded promising. I glance at the shirts and hold out the navy blue one. "This one?"

Their heads shake side to side and at the same time they say, "Pink!"

"I love your shirt." It's the first thing out of Sydney's mouth when she climbs into the passenger seat of my car.

"Yeah?" I wait until Nathan and Chloe are settled in the back before I pull away from the dorm.

"Bright colors—pinks, yellows, greens—they make me happy."

Thank you, Tara.

The Hideout is already busy, but we're able to grab a booth close to the bar. Sydney slides in and I follow.

"I'm glad this worked out. I've been looking forward to hanging with you again."

"You have?" Her smile is fucking radiant.

"Well, yeah. I thought I made it clear the other night that I wanted to keep bumping into you."

"I do too." She ducks her head a tad like she might be embarrassed to admit she likes my company. She glances to Nathan and Chloe across from us. "What are we drinking?"

"I'm gonna grab a pitcher. Be right back." I stand. "Want anything else?"

The tip of her tongue comes out to wet her lips. "I'll come with you."

Angling my body to make room for both of us in the cramped space, I lean against the bar. "What do you feel like drinking?"

"Beer is fine."

"Fine is boring."

"Beer is great, then."

"Pitcher of the IPA on tap," I say to the bartender and then focus back on Sydney. "You look great."

"It's the dress."

"It's you."

She looks unconvinced. "Don't get me wrong, I like the dress, but you could have worn a T-shirt and jeans and you'd still look great."

"Thank you."

"You don't believe me?"

"Well, I've run into you on campus, at parties, bars." She waves a hand indicating The Hideout. "And you only noticed me when I was in the tightest dress I own and standing a foot away from you. If it hadn't been for Nathan talking to Chloe..."

"I'm sorry I didn't notice you before. It isn't because you

aren't beautiful. I'm sure you were just as stunning all those other times. Last year I did my best to keep my head down and focus. Yeah, I went out and partied, but I was living in a fog. I'm convinced of that more than ever now that I know we were in the same room and my eyes failed me."

"You're forgiven."

Back at the table, the four of us chat—me and Sydney more than Nathan and Chloe. They're obviously into one another, but they're a lot more subtle than we are. I dig that about Sydney. She doesn't make me second-guess whether or not she wants to be here. Her attention is solely focused on me and mine on her.

I wrap an arm around the back of the booth, fingertips brushing her shoulder. I refill my glass and take a small drink. "So, did you have a boyfriend last year?"

"No." Her face scrunches up adorably. "Why?"

"Wishful thinking, I guess." Though even as I say it, I get a little rage-y picturing her with someone else. "I'd like to think I only overlooked you because you were on some guy's arm and I was being respectful."

"Does having a boyfriend really stop guys from checking out girls?"

"Well, no, but it usually stops us from doing anything about it. Maybe I looked across the room and you looked happy and content with some guy and I sighed and reluctantly let you be. Being the bigger man and all that."

Her body shakes with laughter. "What about you? As far as I know, you haven't had any girlfriends at Valley, but there was a rumor about you and the women's tennis coach."

"Say what?"

"Gotcha! But have you seen her? She's seriously hot."

Before I know it, Sydney's pulled out her phone and navigating to the Valley U athletics page to show me. And damn, Coach Ryan is hot. Not as hot as Sydney, but definitely hot. Somehow that leads us down a rabbit hole of passing her phone back and forth rating the hotness of all the coaches.

"Are you two ready?" Nathan asks.

I glance up and notice the pitcher is empty. Shit, I have no idea how long Sydney and I have been in our own little bubble.

"Yeah." I look to her. "You want to come back to The White House?"

"Definitely."

When we get back to the house, we find Datson already back from the Prickly Pear and playing Xbox in the living room.

"Oh, man, that's old school. What game is that?" Sydney walks right in and sits down on the couch.

"Tecmo Bowl. It's awesome." I tip my head at Datson. "I demand a rematch from this afternoon. You want winner, Payne?"

He shakes his head. "Gonna hang with my girl."

Chloe and Nathan join us despite acting like they want to be alone. I'm seated next to Sydney. She leans forward watching the game with rapt interest. I get a little too distracted with her beside me. The feel of her leg resting next to mine, the smell of her hair—coconut, I think. I'd really like my hands back—they're itching to touch her.

"Damn. I've never seen anyone lose so fast." Datson punches me in the arm and then looks to Nathan. "You're up."

Nathan lifts a hand. "Shaw, toss me the controller."

I do and then focus my attention on Sydney.

"You're terrible." Those dark eyes are lit with laughter at my loss.

"It's an old game, I'm still getting the hang of it."

She doesn't look convinced. I lay a palm on her thigh and squeeze playfully. "Let's see how you do."

Her gaze goes to my hand and then back to my face. "Bring it on, Tanner."

"Me and Sydney have next game," I tell the guys and then lean closer to Sydney. "You're the only person who calls me that. Well, besides my family."

"Should I call you Shaw?"

"Nah, I like it." I stroke her smooth skin lightly with my thumb, not moving my hand up to creeper level but exploring the chemistry between us. As I expected, it's off the charts.

After video games, where I may or may not have *let* her win (cough, cough, I did not, she beat me straight up), we head out to the pool. Sydney didn't have a suit so she's in one of my shirts and boxers. Nathan and I show the girls how to play water ball. What is usually an intense competition between guys is more of a friendly, flirty game. Sydney and I use every opportunity to touch and splash one another. After we score, she throws her arms around my neck and squeals in victory.

We're killing them. Sydney is as competitive as I am and knowing that every score is another chance that she might hug me in celebration makes me an impossible man to beat. I'm good with incentives.

"All right, we give," Nathan says after the second game. "We're going in to watch a movie or something."

Code, they're going to make out.

"Thanks for the game." I wrap my arms around Sydney's waist underwater and pull her against me. "Are you good staying out here for a while?" I ask her as they climb out and start toward the house. "I love it out here at night."

"Definitely." She leans her head back against my shoulder.

The water is perfect in the warm night air. Clear skies mean there's even a few stars out.

She sighs. "This house, this pool, it's amazing. I'm insanely jealous."

"You have a standing invitation."

"Do you think your roommates would object if I started coming over every day to use this pool?" She swims away from me and then turns over on her back, floating and staring up at the sky.

"Nah, we're pretty good with hot girls showing up to use the pool whenever they want."

She tilts her head to look at me and snorts. "Of course."

I skim my hand through the water and interlock our fingers, using the leverage to pull her back to me. Water drips from her hair down her face and lands on the corner of her mouth. With the pad of my thumb, I wipe it away and then slowly bring my lips to hers.

Chapter Four

SYDNEY

My heart is beating so fast I'm certain Tanner can feel it as I lace my fingers behind his neck and press my body against his. His kiss is tender at first. Soft lips and a gentle touch of his thumb at my chin. As I arch into him and tilt my head, he takes the opportunity to deepen the kiss.

There's a niggling doubt in the back of my mind that worries me we're moving too fast, but everything with Tanner feels so natural. Honestly tonight didn't feel like a first date. It's like I've known him forever.

He inches back and we stare into each other's eyes, chests rising and falling with labored breaths. "Do you want to go inside?"

Nodding, I press my lips back to his and tighten my grip on him. It's so easy to get carried away with him. His fingers slide underneath my shirt to my lower back and he brings our bodies together from chest to knees. An excited shiver shoots up my spine.

His mouth leaves mine and he places warm, wet kisses to

my neck. He shifts and his dick, thick and hard, grazes my sensitive core. It's enough to jolt me back to reality.

"Tanner?"

"Hmmm?" He continues his exploration of my neck with his mouth.

"That feels so good." My eyes close and I reach for my resolve, barely grasping it. "Wait. I need to tell you something before this goes any farther."

Peeling his lips away, he straightens, and his brows raise slightly. "You're married with three kids and a dog named Fido?"

I push at his chest. "No, of course not. The dog's name is Winston, of course."

He smirks.

"I like you a lot and tonight has been... amazing, but I sort of have a five-date rule."

I get a confused stare in response.

"As in, I don't sleep with guys until we've been on five dates." I cringe a bit. There's really no good way to tell someone that you're not down for having sex but you'd like to keep kissing them and maybe rubbing up against them. "It's just, I've done the whole first night hookup, and it's not for me."

"Okay. That's it?"

I nod and smile, thankful to have that out in the open. "I would love to go inside and keep hanging out. Really, tonight has been amazing and I don't want it to end."

"Okay, yeah, cool." He swims to the side and pulls himself up and then holds out a hand to help me.

Later I will replay this scene over and over in my head and think of all the different ways I could and should have worded this conversation. Hindsight is a real bitch.

Tanner and I go in and dry off. I change back into my own clothes and find him splayed out on his bed with his phone in hand. He's in shorts that are low on his hips and a faded basketball T-shirt. When I walk in, he looks up and smiles.

"Ready to show me your skills again?" He sits up and swings his legs over the side of the bed. I'm trying to figure out what he means when he adds, "Datson finally relinquished the Xbox, so it's all ours."

"Oh, yeah, definitely."

He grins and blows by me, flipping the light on the way out. He grabs two beers from the fridge and then we settle into the living room. The house is quiet, and we're the only ones downstairs but we still sit side by side on the couch.

"All right, let's see what you got."

"You know what I got," I taunt. "Do you not remember the last beating I gave you?"

He grunts a response.

For the next two hours, I use more concentration and focus than I have since the time Emily and I challenged some of our teammates to a Just Dance tournament in our dorm room.

I came out on top that night and somehow I do again.

Tanner groans. "Man! I really thought I could beat you this time."

"Because I'm a girl?"

"No, because you said you've never played before." He glances down at my legs. It's the first time since we got out of the pool that he's given any indication that I'm someone he's into. Maybe he's not anymore. "I blame your legs."

"My legs?" I chuckle.

He leans back, resting the controller on his thigh. "They were distracting."

"Maybe *your* legs were distracting me."

We both look to his hairy legs and laugh. Although they are nice—strong and muscular.

"Again?" he asks, nodding to the TV.

"I think I'll stop while I'm ahead."

"I don't blame you." He's quick to his feet and shuts everything off.

"It's late," I say, resigning myself to walking back to my dorm alone in the dark. This night didn't go exactly as I wanted, but I did have fun hanging with Tanner. Hopefully I haven't totally ruined any chance of us doing this again by slowing things down.

He starts toward the stairs and then glances back at me. "Are you coming? You can have my bed, and I'll take the floor."

Fresh hope blooms, but more than anything, I'm happy to spend more time with him.

Inside his room, he takes a pillow and blanket and tosses them to the floor.

"You don't need to do that."

He shrugs and straightens the blanket. "It's fine. I don't mind."

I sit on the edge of the bed. "Seriously, we can sleep in the same bed. Besides, I have all kinds of questions for you."

"Like?" He scoops the pillow up off the floor and falls onto the bed. His big frame bouncing on the mattress makes me fall into the center beside him. We get comfortable laying together with our heads at the bottom of the bed.

"Did you have girlfriends in high school?" I ask.

"One."

"Was it serious?"

"Eh, I guess. We were together for almost a year."

"I'd say a year counts as serious. Why'd it end?"

"Over something stupid." He adjusts the pillow under his head. "She and my sister were both running for student council president and Misty, my girlfriend at the time, lost. She was pissed, lashed out, demanded to know who I voted for and when I wouldn't tell her, she ended it."

"Did you vote for her?"

"A man's vote is private and personal." His eyes twinkle as his lips twitch with humor.

"So, you voted for your sister and your girlfriend got pissed and dumped you?"

"She *assumed* I voted for my sister, but yeah."

"Rough."

We lay there in silence for a few moments. I try to picture him in high school cheering on his sister like a good big brother.

"You're close to your sister then?"

He smiles. "She's a pain in the ass."

"I'll take that as a yes."

He laughs. "Yeah, we're close. She's just a year younger than me, goes to college in Utah. Do you have any siblings?"

"No, only child. I used to wish for a sister."

"Funny, I used to wish I was an only child. Especially when Tara was playing jokes on me or trying to tag along with my friends."

"What's she like? Is she into sports like you?"

"Yeah, we both played a bunch of different sports growing up. Our parents were big on getting us out of the house and active. She's only playing soccer now, but she was pretty good at basketball too."

"That's cool."

"She'd like you."

I'm not sure what makes him think that, but it makes me

smile. "I'm sure I'd like her too. Especially since it sounds like she enjoys picking on her big brother."

He grins. "What about you? Any boyfriends?"

"A few in high school, none that lasted very long."

"How come?" He touches a strand of my hair that's splayed out near his hand, wrapping it around his index finger.

"I was a little bit fickle and I had a habit of jumping in before I got to know them, and once I did..."

With a smirk, he pulls my hair lightly. "You didn't like what you found."

"Something like that."

"Is that why you threw up the block downstairs earlier when I kissed you?"

I feel the blush creep up my neck and my ears burn. "Let me explain—"

"Nah, it's cool. I don't usually jump into things so quickly either. I mean, I've hooked up with girls and done the one-night stand thing..." He stops and makes a face. "I'm doing a terrible job of explaining, but what I'm trying to say is that even though we don't know each other very well yet, you seem like a cool chick. I feel so comfortable with you, like we've known each other a really long time."

"Same." I scoot closer to him, prepared to kiss him and make up for pulling away earlier. I may not be ready to have sex with him, but kissing... I want more of that.

He wraps his arms around me and pulls me into his chest. I breathe him in. He smells like laundry soap and chlorine and something that's just him.

He pulls back and I tilt my head up and lean in. "I'm really glad I met you," he says and bops me on the nose. "Ready to sleep?"

I pause and he climbs up the bed and pulls down the

covers. I get underneath and he goes to turn off the light and then gets in on the other side. He pulls off his T-shirt and tosses it on the floor, then lays down.

My eyes have barely closed when he says, "Tell me about these times you allegedly saw me last year."

"I thought you wanted to sleep."

"Bedtime stories, babe."

"What do you want to know?" I ask with a laugh.

"The usual stuff. Where were we, who were you with, how hot did I look, what were you wearing?"

I open my eyes to find his face not far from mine and a huge grin on it. "Let's see, I saw you at The Hideout a few times, here…" If I thought long enough I could probably tell him every single time, in order. The details are harder to remember off hand, but that feeling of excitement and hope that it was the night we'd finally talk is the same feeling I have now. Being with Tanner is exhilarating.

"You forgot the most important part of the story."

"You looked hot," I assure him.

"Of course I did, but the most important question was what were *you* wearing?"

"Oh, I didn't forget. I wasn't wearing any clothes, I was naked."

His eyes darken and his jaw ticks before I start laughing.

"You're so gullible."

Big, warm hands find my waist under the covers and tickle my ribs and sides. I jump and squirm to get away, but he holds me tight and continues his onslaught. "Stop, oh man, stop. I'm so ticklish and I will so get you back for this." I'm not sure how much of my words can be understood as I squeak and laugh. I manage to elbow him in the chest and he finally quits but doesn't stop touching me.

"Turn around."

"You think I'm going to turn my back to you? No way, I'm keeping my eyes where I can see your hands."

"I won't tickle you anymore. Come on, turn around, I want to cuddle."

I comply, half-convinced he's joking, but he pulls me tight against his chest and sighs.

"I didn't picture you as a cuddler."

"I am the *best* cuddler."

"Says who?" My eyes flutter closed, and I revel in the feel of him wrapped around me. "You do this often?"

"Says me and no, now shh."

"You're very bossy."

His grip squeezes around my middle. We breathe together and my body goes limp, happy and content and finally tired.

"'Night, Tanner."

"'Night, babe."

Chapter Five

"Sydney's coming over again?" Datson has a smug smile on his face. "You two are like a thing now, huh?"

"Not exactly."

"Why not? She's pretty hot."

"*Pretty* hot? You need your eyes checked." I hit the bill of his hat as I hurry to answer the door.

I pull it wide and Sydney stands there, phone to her ear, in a bright blue dress, blonde hair pulled up in a ponytail. Jesus, every time I see this girl, she legit takes my breath away.

Her eyes meet mine and she mouths hello while walking inside.

"Okay, Mom, I've got to go now. I just walked into a friend's house." She tilts her head side to side impatiently while I imagine her mom keeps talking. She smiles at me, but I'm stuck on the word *friend*.

It's been two weeks since she stayed over the first time and we've hung out or talked almost every day. Things are easy between us and fun. So much fun. She said she wanted to take things slow and I'm good with that, but how long do I wait to make a move?

I scold myself, not for the first time. I can be patient. Very, very patient. The bits of information I've pulled from her about her past relationships have made her untrusting. I want to restore that trust, not just because I want to sleep with her but because she deserves that.

"Sorry," she says after ending the call. "My mom babbles on the phone. I can barely get a word in."

"Like mother like daughter."

"Punk." She takes a seat in the living room. "What are we doing tonight?"

"Oh, uh." I glance down at my shorts and bare feet. Sydney's dressed to kill, per the usual. "Did you want to go out?"

"Well, we could stay in and I could kick your ass at Tecmo Bowl again, your choice." She kicks off her sandals and pulls her feet under her.

Let's see, keep her to myself and only a fifteen second jog to my bed in case tonight is the night or go out where I'll have to share her with a bunch of other people? Easy call.

"Don't get ahead of yourself, babe. I've been practicing." I hand her a remote and settle back, ready to redeem myself.

As they always do, the hours go by too quickly. Nathan comes home, stopping in the living room. "Hey, what's up?"

"Losing." I groan as Sydney wins again. "How am I so bad at this game?"

Nathan chuckles. "You really are terrible."

I really am. "What are you doing back so early?" I ask him.

"Early? It's after midnight."

Sydney and I share a shocked look and then both laugh. I

sit up and my body protests. "Shit, I guess we haven't moved in a while."

"I should get home." She stands and slips on her shoes. "I have to give a speech tomorrow morning."

Nathan heads off. "'Night, guys."

"Let me grab a shirt and shoes and I'll walk you."

Sydney and I make our way to campus slowly. It isn't far, but by unspoken agreement, we stretch out our time together.

"What's your speech about?"

She hooks her arm through mine. "We have to give a five-minute speech that teaches the class something. Something that we're interested in and bonus points for uniqueness."

"Oh man, I can't wait to hear this."

"Mine is about organizing clothes and accessories in dorm-sized closets."

"I should have known it was related to your clothes somehow." I pull at the soft cotton material of her dress. "I like this one."

"Thanks." She glances over at me. "I thought it matched the color of your eyes."

"Yeah?" I think that's a compliment. I know how much she likes her dresses though, and she has a whole bunch of them, so maybe each of them reminds her of something and her noting a dress matches my eye color is just a normal thing for her. This girl has me questioning all sorts of things that I never imagined I'd give a second thought.

I go with her inside Freddy dorm and up to her floor.

"Thanks for walking me home."

"Thanks for coming to see me. Maybe tomorrow we can go out, like actually leave the house and do something?" My hands are a little sweaty and I shove them in my pockets.

"Can't. We have a team dinner thing and Saturday I

promised Emily we'd go to the football party. You could come with us if you want."

I like her friends, but I'd far prefer to spend the night with just her. Maybe a movie or dinner, or the bar. "Okay, yeah, whatever you want."

Her wide smile makes me forget to be disappointed. "I'll text you when I know what everyone's doing."

Tipping back on my heels, that disappointment creeps back in knowing that we're not going to be able to hang out for a couple of days. And I really hate this weird place we're in. Most of the time I don't notice it because I'm too busy enjoying her company, but when we say goodbye there's always this beat of awkwardness. When can I see her again? Should I kiss her? Have we hung out enough times that she trusts me?

Sydney smiles tentatively, hand on the doorknob. A war wages in my head.

Kiss her.

Don't freak her out.

Fucking kiss her already.

You'll know when the time is right.

It feels pretty fucking right.

While I'm still debating, Sydney makes the decision for me. She steps forward, kisses me on the cheek so quickly I almost miss it, and then throws open her door and goes inside. "Night, Tanner."

How did I get friend zoned by a girl that by her own words had been dying to meet me for an entire year? I think it might have been this moment. I should have taken her out to a party or to dinner. I should have kissed her. Literally anything would have been better than what I did, which was nothing.

Chapter Six

SYDNEY

Present day - two years later

"Tanner?" I call as I walk through the front door. My voice echoes in the big, quiet space. I move through to the back of the house to see if he's outside and then backtrack to go upstairs. Everyone else has already gone home for summer break, and if it weren't for Tanner's car out front and the text he sent me five minutes ago, I'd think he was gone too.

As I ascend the stairs, I finally hear him. Above the sound of the shower, he sings. The words and tempo don't match any song I know, but he keeps right on belting it out. The bathroom door is cracked open and steam seeps out.

"It sounds like you're drowning a cat in there," I say, standing along the wall so I don't accidentally get an eyeful. If there's anything I've learned being friends with Tanner over the last two years, it's that he's unabashedly proud of his body and not afraid who sees it. Modesty? What's that?

The water stops, and I hear him push the shower curtain open. "There's a pussy joke in there somewhere."

Rolling my eyes, but smiling all the same, I step back when his footsteps approach. "Are you decent?"

"Always."

"Is your dick covered?"

He chuckles and moves past me. He's dripping water all over the hallway, but he does have a towel wrapped around his waist.

I follow him into his room and sit on his bed. He steps into his closet, tosses the towel out onto the floor, and when he reappears, he has on a pair of shorts.

He drops beside me on the mattress. "How was your meeting with the trainer?"

I fall onto my back with a dramatic sigh. "Awful. She squashed any hope that I can play this summer. Seriously, I'm fine." I lift my arm and rotate until I feel the pinch in my shoulder. Okay, fine is a stretch but the tournament in Brazil isn't for another three weeks. I'll be fine by then. Mostly fine. I really wanted to spend my summer by the beach.

"Sorry, babe. You don't want to take any chances before senior year, though. Better to rest it and be ready in the fall."

"Yeah, yeah," I grumble. That's almost exactly what the doctor said. It doesn't make missing out on a summer of traveling and playing volleyball suck any less. I turn onto my side to face Tanner. "When are you leaving?"

"I was planning on heading out this afternoon." He rakes a hand through his wet hair.

I nod and resign myself to a summer of boredom in my hometown. I haven't been back home for an entire summer since I came to college and there's a very good reason for that. The small town where I grew up is charming and quaint and all those things people talk up about small towns, but it's also super dull. No beach, no mountains, no good places to shop. Most of my friends from high school have moved away or are married with kids. It's going to be the longest summer ever.

"Hey." He nudges me. "How about I stay tonight and we hang out?"

"And do what? Everyone is gone."

"Since when have we ever needed other people to have a good time?"

The corners of my mouth pull into a small smile. He's right. Tanner and I can (and have) found ways to have fun regardless of what everyone else is doing. If the party is lame, we'll still make sure we have a good time. It's one of my favorite things about our friendship, he makes everything better.

"Okay, yeah, if you're sure you can stay. I don't want to keep you from whatever plans you have for the awesome summer you keep talking about."

He cocks a brow.

"Okay, fine, screw your awesome summer. Stay and hang out with me." I push out my lower lip and his eyes crinkle at the corners. When Tanner smiles, really smiles, it's as clear in his eyes as it is his lips.

"Done." He sits up. "I need to pack, though, so I can leave first thing in the morning."

"You start packing and I'll grab drinks."

The guys' fridge is the emptiest I've ever seen it and the liquor on the counter is sad, too. I grab a bottle of Malibu and four Natty Lights and head back upstairs.

Tanner makes a face when I hand him one of the cheap beers.

"It's all you had, but I grabbed this too."

His expression only sours more. "Malibu?"

"I like it."

"You're the only one. It's been down there since our last party."

"This is the same one?" I asked surprised. Tanner, despite all his eye rolling, always makes sure they have Malibu and Coke on hand for me. His preferences are Jager and beers that are too hoppy for my liking. For a college kid, he has expensive tastes that I like to tease him about.

He opens his beer and takes a long drink, grimaces, and then takes another long gulp. He crushes the can in his hand and my brows raise.

"Only take about thirty more of those to get me drunk. It's basically water."

"Take a shot," I say and unscrew the top of the Malibu. My eyes widen with an idea. "Every time you complain about the beer, you have to take a shot."

He does and then hands it back and grabs his second beer. "Fine, but every time you complain that I'm packing all wrong, you have to take a shot."

I glance at his open suitcase on the bed. His jeans are tossed in and a couple pairs of shoes. He's already pulled out a second suitcase in preparation for filling the first.

I can't help myself, I cross the room and grab the jeans, roll them, and then tuck them back inside. "Look at all the room you could save though."

He chuckles and juts his chin toward the bottle.

Beer in one hand and Malibu in the other, I take a seat on the bed next to his suitcase. Silently, I continue to repack each item he adds. He doesn't comment but shakes his head every time he glances at my handiwork.

He brings a pile of mismatched socks and drops them on top with a knowing smirk.

"Okay, stop."

He raises his hand and makes a triumphant fist. "I wondered what your breaking point would be. If the socks didn't work, I was going to toss my dirty laundry in. Drink up, babe."

"You're the worst."

By the time we're finished, I'm drunk, and Tanner has on his tipsy smile.

"We're going to need more booze," I tell him as we head downstairs. Without warning, I wrap my arms around his neck from behind and jump. He catches me and carries me piggyback into the kitchen.

"Nah, we're good." He goes to the pantry and pulls down a box with alcohol in it. "I was going to take this with me."

"You're just now mentioning this?"

"Someone needed to drink the gross beer left in the fridge." He shudders. "This is my reward."

"Shot," I tell him.

He pulls out a bottle of Jager and I groan, but at least we're done packing, so I don't have to worry about holding up my end on the shot-taking bargain. I'm in a happy drunk state now but another couple of shots and I'll be passed out. He brings us into the kitchen, and I drop down and take a seat on one of the barstools.

"Here, mix this with some soda water so you don't pass out on me." He puts the vodka in front of me.

"You know me too well."

We make our drinks and take them outside. It's hot, but I didn't bring my bathing suit, so we sit on the edge of the pool and dangle our feet in.

"What's Amelia doing this summer?"

"Ah, shit." Tanner pulls out his phone and winces. "She still thinks I'm coming tonight."

"I thought you were going to the lake?"

"Yeah, I am, but I told her I'd stop at her house on the way through and we could grab dinner."

"Oh."

"Be right back." He stands with the phone to his ear. "Hey, I'm sorry..." His voice trails off as he retreats inside.

I get up off the ground and go sit in the shade. A pit of guilt sits heavy in my stomach. It isn't like I knew, but I still feel bad. This happens a lot with Tanner and me. We hang out and the rest of the world fades away which inevitably leads to one of us forgetting about something we were supposed to do.

It's one of the reasons I haven't dated that much since we met. I hate that look of disappointment guys get when I tell them I'm going to hang with Tanner. They never understand our friendship. One of the requirements for any guy I date is that he needs to get along with my best friend. I may be single forever.

Tanner has dated a lot more than I have over the years and I've tried my best to make his girlfriends feel comfortable. Amelia, his latest girlfriend, seems nice. A little quiet and reserved for him, but if she makes him happy, then that's all that matters.

He blows out a long breath and takes a seat in a lounge chair next to me. "Well, that could have gone better."

"Sorry. Is she really pissed?"

"No, worse, disappointed."

"This is all my fault. Maybe I should text her."

"No." He holds his arm out to stop me. "No offense, babe, but texting her is probably the worst thing you could do."

"But it isn't your fault. You wouldn't have stayed if it weren't for me. You were being a good friend."

"She doesn't see it like that."

I feel awful and the buzz I had seems to have worn off. "Is there any way you can still make it?"

"No, that ship has sailed." He lifts the Jager bottle and takes a drink. He nudges me. "It'll be fine. Don't worry."

I'm not so sure but stating that seems the opposite of helpful. "You're right. I'm sure you'll charm your way back into her good graces."

"I don't do that." He smiles.

I cock a brow and he chuckles and passes over the Jager.

"Drink, babe. New rule, every time you look at me like you feel sorry for me, you have to take a shot."

"No way. I'd walk around drunk all the time." Still, I take a small drink, scowl at the black licorice taste, and hand it back. "Do you think our lives would be easier, dating-wise, if we weren't friends?"

It's something I've thought about a lot over the past year. I think I'm finally at that point where I feel ready to be in a serious relationship, but I worry as soon as I bring them around to hang out with Tanner, they'll start acting weird, or worse, it'd put a wedge between me and him. We've never had serious relationships at the same time. Would we double date? I can't picture it.

I glance over at my best friend, hoping he'll ease my mind, but he shrugs. "Maybe."

I lean my head back against the lounge chair and shut my eyes.

"Hey, look at me."

I open my lids to find Tanner has sat up and swiveled his legs around so he's closer. "Screw everyone else. You're my person, and if Amelia can't understand that then it's already doomed to fail."

"Tanner—"

"No, I'm serious."

"I know, but I don't want to be the reason you and Amelia don't work."

"Tonight was my fault. It's on me." He grabs my hand and squeezes. "Got it?"

I nod. "Yeah."

"Now, help me figure out how I'm going to make it right with Amelia."

"Oooh, I love when you screw up and we get to make big gestures."

"We?"

"We both know I'm the brain of the operation, you're just the pretty face."

"You think my face is pretty?" He tilts his face side to side showing off with a smug smile.

"We don't have time to feed your ego and come up with a plan."

"Good point." He stands and helps me to my feet. "We need food."

"I'll order pizza, you start making a list of things she likes."

Chapter Seven

TANNER

The sound of the TV and the end credits of the movie wakes me. The side of my face sticks to the leather couch as I try to sit up. Sydney's using my ass as a pillow. She groans and then her big, brown eyes meet mine.

"I love that movie. It's my favorite." Her voice is thick with sleep.

"Obviously."

"Shut it." She sits tall and rolls her neck. She's so freaking gorgeous. It hits me at the weirdest times. Years ago, when it was clear Sydney and I were going to be just friends, I made the decision to stop looking at her like that and enjoy what we had—an awesome friendship. I know that sounds like it would be hard, but when it came down to it, I knew it was either see her as a friend or lose her.

I couldn't bear that. I mean who else would stay up half the night coming up with a list of ideas to smooth things over with Amelia? Still, sometimes, it just hits me that my best friend is a knockout.

I wince as I hear Amelia's disappointed voice in my head.

I'm not sure anything Sydney and I came up with will work. It isn't the first time that I lost track of time and accidentally blew her off to hang with Sydney.

Still, Amelia is great, and I want to make it up to her.

"I'm going to bed. Are you coming?"

Sydney's eyes briefly flit over my bare chest. "I'll sleep down here. It's fine."

"Come on, don't be silly." I stand but she doesn't budge.

"I was thinking while I was sleeping—"

"You were thinking while you were sleeping?"

"Hush." She closes her thumb and fingers on her right hand to mimic a shushing motion. "I was thinking, maybe we should stop hanging out so much or at least not do things I know will make Amelia uncomfortable."

"What?"

"We've always said, screw everyone else. If they can't deal with it, it's their problem, but maybe it should be our problem." Her face is stoic and dead serious which makes something in my chest ache. "We're going to be apart this summer anyway. Maybe it'll be good for both of us. Amelia is nice and I want you to be happy."

"Hanging out with you makes me happy. You're my best friend."

"Same." She stands and wraps herself around me. The top of her head comes up just under my chin and I tuck her in close and breathe in her shampoo.

She pulls back first with a big smile. "So, I'll sleep down here."

I scoop her up and throw her over my shoulder. "Don't be dumb. The plan obviously has to start tomorrow. No one makes a plan and executes it on the same day."

She laughs as I start toward the stairs. "Fine, but I'm sleeping on the floor."

"Whatever you want, babe."

The next morning when I wake up, Sydney's already gone. I grab my phone and read her text.

Sydney: Have a great summer. Don't forget the roses for Amelia!!

After showering and loading up my car, I get on the road. It's only about two hours to Amelia's hometown which will have me arriving right around lunchtime.

My phone rings from the console. I take it and press speaker. "Hey."

"Hey," Tara's chipper voice replies. "Are you at the lake?"

"Nah, not yet. I should be there late this afternoon."

"I'm so jealous." Her dramatic sigh makes me chuckle.

"That's what you get for taking classes during the summer. Super lame, T."

"Yeah, yeah. We can't all be career jocks. Speaking of, did you give any more thought to our conversation about focusing on just one next year?"

An uncomfortable knot forms in my chest and I shift in the driver's seat. "Of course, I've thought about it."

"I know you love playing both basketball and baseball, but if you put all your energy to one, it makes it more likely you'll go higher in the draft and it frees up more time for a real life. That last picture Amelia posted on Instagram of your date night was pathetic. You don't even leave the house for dates now?" I get another giant sigh.

"We had a good time. We watched all her favorite movies and ordered a ton of food. She said it was awesome."

"She lied."

I don't really think that's the case, but I know better than to argue with my sister on what women do and don't want.

"What do your coaches say, or your teammates? And Amelia, what does she say? She shuts me down any time I bring it up, but I know it must be hard for her. I can't be the only one who thinks you're crazy to do this another year?"

Amelia hasn't voiced any concerns to me, but I haven't really asked her opinion either.

"Maybe not just another year. It's possible I could keep doing both after college."

"You're serious?"

"It's been done before."

"Yeah, but Tanner, what kind of life is that? Not just for you, but for a family?"

The low battery notification comes up on my phone. "My phone is going to die, and my charger is buried in one of my bags. Can you call me back later to yell at me about this?"

"I'm sorry." A little of the fight in her voice dies. "I just don't want you to forget to have a life while trying to be some sort of super jock."

"I won't. I'm not. I have a life. An awesome one. One that's going to the lake this summer, unlike you."

"Ha! All right, fine. I'm temporarily satisfied, but I'm calling you back tonight because I want to talk about our plans for the Fourth this year. Is Amelia going with you today?"

"She's coming up for the week of the Fourth and maybe one more weekend. She's working at her parents' insurance office this summer."

"I can't wait to see her again. You two are so cute together. Okay, talk later. Drive safe."

I swear she's more of a mother hen than our mother.

When I get close to Amelia's, I swing by to get her flowers and then head to her parents' house. I haven't met her mom or dad yet, so I'm grateful they're at work. I don't want the first time I meet them to be when I'm digging myself out of a hole.

But Amelia throws open the door with a smile and then launches herself at me, crushing the roses between us.

"Hey," I get out with a mouthful of her hair. "You smashed my apology."

She pulls back, glances down at the roses, and then kisses me. I guess that means apology accepted. Points for Sydney.

Inside her house, we sit on the couch in the living room. It's a nice place, homey, well taken care of, lots of photos of Amelia and her sister, Beth. Her close relationship with her sister is one of the things we bonded over. Family is important to us.

And my sister and girlfriend get along, so that's a bonus. I brought Amelia home with me for a quick trip to celebrate my parents' anniversary and Tara quickly befriended her.

"I'm really sorry about last night. Sydney was bummed about her shoulder, and I offered to stay before I thought it through."

"It's okay. I'm just glad you're here now, and we'll have more time this summer just the two of us."

Slowly, I nod. "Yeah, that's what Sydney said."

"Really?" Her brows furrow together. "I'm surprised she hasn't found a way to invite herself along to the lake." I don't understand the bitterness in her tone. Sydney's always been great to her.

"Come on, Sydney doesn't do that."

Amelia pauses waiting for... something.

"She doesn't," I insist.

"Oh my god, you're totally oblivious."

"To?"

"Sydney is in love with you."

"No, she isn't. I've told you before, we've only ever been friends. It isn't like that between us." Minus one hot kiss, but this is not the time to bring that up. I tried full-on honesty with the first girlfriend I had after Sydney and I became friends, and that just made her that much more leery.

"You're blind."

"No, I'm not. Listen, we actually talked last night about giving each other some space so it would make you more comfortable. Sydney is on your side. Whose idea do you think it was to bring roses?"

"So..." She pauses, deep in thought. "You told Sydney you wanted some space, for us? And she was cool with it?"

"The whole thing was her idea. She said she wants us to be happy."

I wait for the relief to show on her face, maybe a smile. Instead she looks sad.

"This isn't going to work."

Well, that's unexpected. "What are you talking about?"

"I can't believe I didn't see it," she mumbles under her breath. She gets to her feet and I follow her, not realizing we're at the front door and she's seeing me out until we're standing in the entryway. "All this time I thought it was Sydney that was in love with you, but it's the other way around, isn't it?"

My brain is tripping along trying to catch up.

Amelia crosses her arms over her chest. "You're in love with Sydney."

Her words slam into me and my first instinct is to deny, but she doesn't give me a chance.

Unfolding her arms, she opens the front door. "Goodbye, Tanner."

I'm still wrapping my head around what the fuck just happened when I pull back onto the freeway. I call Sydney.

"Hey," her bubbly voice answers. "How'd it go?"

"Great," I say. "I mean, not great but it's fine. Are you still at Valley?"

"Yeah, I am packing now, should be on the road in fifteen minutes or so. Back home for the summer." Her voice sounds defeated as she says the last part.

"Good. Stay put. I'm coming to get you."

"Uhh, what?"

"You're coming with me to the lake this summer. I'll explain everything when I get there."

It takes very little convincing to get Sydney to agree, and as soon as she does and we pile her bags into the back of my car, I feel lighter than I have in months. In love with Sydney? I shake my head. I left that part out of the replay I gave Sydney. The important thing is, we broke up and that Amelia isn't the right one for me.

Sydney thought we needed space to make Amelia happy and I think I need someone who can accept that I'm not going to pretend she isn't important to me just because they're insecure. Plus, the best way to get over a broken heart... or a wounded one, if I'm totally transparent, is to hang with Sydney.

Two years, Sydney has had my back. Through girlfriends, the loss of my grandpa, fights with teammates, bad grades— you name it, she's always been there to support me. I'm not tossing her over for a girl. Another girl.

"This is going to be the best summer ever," I tell her, glancing over as she pulls on a pair of sunglasses. "Four weeks with no cares in the world. And my sister is coming up for Fourth of July weekend with a couple of her friends. We do it up big every year. There's nowhere better than the lake for the Fourth."

"I can't believe after all this time I still haven't met her. Thank you for this. I'm sorry about Amelia, though."

"It wasn't meant to be."

And honestly, I'm more excited about the next month knowing Sydney's going to be there. My original plan was to spend all of June at the lake by myself. My family has a house there that largely goes unused. My parents bought the place a few years ago in anticipation of retirement, but neither of them have retired yet which means Tara and I are the ones who use it most.

Amelia was going to come down for the last week so we could spend the holiday together before I head back to Valley for basketball camp, but this is even better. Four weeks on the water, kicking back, and enjoying my last real summer with my favorite person.

Next year I'll have to worry about the real world and the responsibilities that come after graduation. But not this summer.

It's dusk when we finally get to the lake. We stop at the

grocery store and grab enough food and alcohol to get us through a few days, and then we're pulling up to the house.

"Wow, Tanner, when you said that you had a place at the lake, I was picturing a condo or, well, something a lot less house than this."

"It's three bedrooms, three bath—basically big enough for the whole family to stay. That was important to my parents when they were looking for real estate out here. I think they're hoping we can keep spending time out here even once Tara and I graduate." I grab the bags from the back. "Come on, I'll show you the best part."

We go in through the garage and I drop the groceries in the kitchen and usher Sydney to the living room. It's too dark to get the full effect, but Sydney still gasps beside me.

"Right?"

"Tanner, this is amazing. Holy shit. Are you sure it's cool that I'm here?"

"Definitely."

I watch as she scans the horizon and takes it all in. Her blonde hair is wild from the drive up with the windows down and her brown eyes are wide with excitement. Totally worth the entire trip to see her this excited.

The lake is lit up with boats. The moon shines down over the water and there's a faint lull from the boat motors.

"Tomorrow, I'll take you out on the boat, but it's pretty killer sitting out there at night if you're up for dinner and drinks on the deck."

"Definitely. What can I do to help?"

"I need to turn on the water and check around the place, then I'll cook. Grab a drink and relax. I'll join you when I can."

She doesn't need me to tell her twice. She has a Malibu and

Coke poured and is padding outside before I even get the groceries put away.

Tara calls as I'm pulling the toasted raviolis out of the oven and putting them on a plate.

"Hey, what's up?" I hold the phone between my ear and shoulder and grab a mostly still warm beer from the fridge.

"Did you make it to the lake?"

I twist off the cap and toss it in the trash. "Yep, just got in about twenty minutes ago."

"Ah, I'm so jealous. Stupid summer school."

The sliding glass door opens and Sydney steps into the dining room with an empty glass.

"Do you want another drink, babe?" I ask away from the phone.

"I got it." She snags a toasted rav on her way to the fridge.

"Is that Amelia?" my sister asks excitedly. "Did you convince her to come up sooner?"

"Nah, Sydney's with me."

"What about Amelia?"

"We broke up."

"In the five hours since I've talked to you, you've managed to break up with one girl and replace her with another? Jesus, Tanner," my sister admonishes. "Insensitive much? I need to call Amelia and check on her."

"It's just Sydney, and Amelia's fine. She broke up with me."

"Not without reason, I'm sure. You were so good together. She was nice and decent." She sighs and then her voice softens. "What happened?"

"Can we talk about this later?" I glance at Sydney and force a smile.

"Yes. Are you okay?"

"Never better."

Sydney makes another drink and takes it and the plate of raviolis out to the deck.

"I gotta go. I'm starving and Sydney's about to eat all the toasted ravioli. I'll call you next week to hash out plans for the Fourth, and I'll see you in a few weeks with my sweet summer tan."

"Jerk," she says playfully. "Bye T."

I pocket my phone and hustle outside. The sun has almost completely disappeared, and the only sound is the water lapping and the boats speeding by. I love everything about being on the lake. The heat of the sun out on the boat, zipping around on jet skis, party cove, but sitting outside after dark chilling with a drink in hand, might be my favorite.

Taking a seat next to Sydney, I raise my beer. "Cheers to the best summer ever."

Chapter Eight

SYDNEY

When I wake up it takes a few seconds to remember where I am. Smiling, I throw back the comforter and pad across the hall to the master bedroom where Tanner is spread out face down on the king-size bed.

"Wake up." I bounce onto the bed. "It's after nine."

He groans. "We're on lake time. Nothing good happens before noon."

Still, he turns over, hair mussed and face lined from the pillow. His gaze drops to my chest and over my body and he smirks. "You're already in your suit?"

"I slept in it." I get up on my knees and bounce. "Get up. Get up."

He grabs me around the waist and pulls me down beside him. "Five more minutes."

His hold tightens and I'm caught between his arms and his chest and his very hard dick. It's an important rule of Tanner's and my friendship not to point out things like this. While we have no problem showing a little skin from time to time— changing clothes in front of one another and the like—noting his morning wood is one of those things I just let go. Still, I'm all too aware of it.

Squirming, I wriggle out of his hold and get to my feet beside the bed. "I'm going to get ready. If you're not up by the time I'm done, I'm going without you." It's an empty threat, but one that I know will get him moving.

I brush my hair into a ponytail, spray on sunscreen, slip on my shoes, and grab my sunglasses. The shower's running in the master bathroom which means Tanner is up. I grab water and head outside to the deck.

Despite what Tanner said about lake time, there are already boats on the water. In the daylight, I can see so much more than the lake though. There's a trail behind the house where people are walking and jogging. The houses on either side have a similar setup with a deck overlooking the wide expanse of water. It looks like several houses share a dock. Either that or Tanner's family has a lot of boats.

"Do you want me to bring the Malibu in the cooler?" Tanner walks out carrying the cooler and sets it on the wood deck. "I've got water, beer, and Coke in here." Without waiting for my response, he tosses it in. "Eh, let's bring it."

"What about food?"

"Knew I forgot something." He winks. "Kidding, I packed plenty of food."

I can barely contain my excitement as we walk down to the dock. My knowledge of boats is basically nonexistent, but this one is nice. Aside from the seat behind the wheel, there's a bench at the back big enough for three people and at the front there's two more seats.

Tanner gets everything situated. I offer to help, but it's clear pretty quickly that it's going to take him longer to explain to me how to help than to just do it himself.

As we pull away from the dock, my body hums with excitement. The morning sun has already warmed the air, but as we pick up speed, goose bumps dot my arms.

Tanner smiles, looking more at peace than I've ever seen him, as he drives the boat. If he's upset about Amelia, I can't tell.

I have no idea where we're going, but I don't care. I sit back and let the serenity of the lake wash over me.

I'm not sure how much time passes while he takes me across the lake, or maybe around it, I've lost all sense of direction. The boat slows and he turns to face me with a big grin on his face. "Beer me."

I grab two from the cooler and hand him one. He pulls out koozies from a storage area and then life vests.

"Grab one of those and let's test the water. Probably freezing, but you have to get a little lake water on you your first time out."

It is cold as we first get in, but we sit on the life jackets and relax with our beer.

"And you said lake time didn't start until noon. I might be drunk by then."

He chuckles. "You can't drink all day if you don't start in the morning."

"So, this is how you spend your summers? Boozing on the lake?"

"Pretty much." He takes a drink. "Actually, there's a lot more to do here. There's a lot of good restaurants and bars along the water. There's a decent golf course a few miles from the house, running trails, and my buddy Jonah lives right next to The Cove. It's a bar and restaurant where they have concerts on Friday nights. We can hear the bands perfectly from his deck. He's got a pool at his place too."

"Who needs a pool?" I dip my head back and let my hair fall into the water. I want to forget everything that led to my being here, but I have a nagging worry that Tanner might need me to be here for him despite dodging any attempt I've made at bringing it up. "Are you okay? Are you sure you don't want to talk about it?"

It takes him a second to realize I'm talking about the breakup with Amelia. "Yeah, I'm fine. It was for the best."

I don't know if that's true, but he seems like he's doing all right, so I give him a pass for now.

We swim a little, mostly just float, until both our beers are empty.

"Now what?" I ask as we climb back onto the boat.

"First weekend on the lake... party cove."

Whatever I expected, party cove is so much more. Rows of boats are lined up and tied together. Boats of all sizes and so many I lose track. Music pumps from a DJ stand at the end of one line.

Tanner pulls up to a huge boat with an upper deck blasting music that competes with that of the DJ. A guy with red hair and black swim trunks comes down to help us tie up.

"Shaw!" he says after the boat's secure. "It's good to see you."

Tanner hops over onto the other boat and they embrace. He holds out his hand and helps me over. "Jonah, this is Sydney."

Jonah grins, looks from me to Tanner and back at me. "This is *the* Sydney?"

"Hey." I wave awkwardly.

He steps forward and crushes me in a hug. He's a big guy, not quite as tall as Tanner but more muscular.

"Sydney, this is my buddy, Jonah."

When he finally frees me, he's still grinning ear to ear. "It's so rad to meet you. I've heard a ton about you. This guy basically never shuts up about you. 'Sydney this, Sydney that.'" He smacks Tanner on the chest. "Come on up, Ollie and a few of the guys from last summer are here too."

Jonah goes ahead and Tanner gives me a sheepish smile. "Ready to meet the lake crew?"

"I'm not sure."

"Good answer. They're a rowdy group, but harmless."

After I'm introduced to everyone, we grab drinks and take a seat on the upper deck. In the short time since I glanced around at party cove, a ton more people have shown up, and as far as I can see, people are standing on their boats drinking and having a good time.

Shots flow as easy as water. Tanner passes, sticking to water or soda since he's driving us back, but I get caught up in the excitement. I'm three shots in, dancing with girls I don't know, and feeling it way more than I usually do when I realize we didn't eat breakfast.

As if he can read my thoughts, Tanner appears with a sandwich.

"Oh, you're a prince." I snatch it from him, still swaying in place, and take a large bite.

He unscrews a cap on the water in his other hand and holds it out to me next.

"Seriously, I don't deserve you."

One of the girls dancing beside me smiles. "Aww, you two are the sweetest." She sticks out her bottom lip. "I wish I had a boyfriend to take care of me."

"He's not my boyfriend," I say around another bite. The bread sticks to the roof of my mouth, making the words hard to understand.

"You two aren't together?" She points from me to Tanner, and we both shake our heads.

A flare of irritation takes over when she steps closer to him and links her arm through his. "Then you have to dance with me."

He resists at first, but she sticks out that lip again. She has nice lips. Big and full, just like her boobs. I glance down at mine and stick out my chest a little more. Even so, mine are nowhere near as big as hers, and I have serious boob envy right now.

I retreat to take a seat and finish my sandwich while Tanner gets pulled farther into the circle of girls moving to the beat.

The food helps, as does the water, but I shake my head when Jonah comes over and offers me another shot.

He hands them off and then plops down beside me. "You know, we were half-convinced he made you up."

"What?"

"Shaw made you sound too good to be true, and none of us had ever met you." He shrugs his big shoulders. "I'm glad you two finally got together."

"Oh, we're not together. We're just friends."

"Really?"

"Really." It isn't anything I haven't heard before. People always assume there's something else going on between me and Tanner. "Is it so hard to believe that a guy and girl can be best friends?"

"Yes. No. I don't know. Normally, I'd say it's totally possi-

ble, but the way he talked about you... shit, it was like he'd
found his soul mate."

My insides feel all squishy. "I feel the same about him. He's
the best."

"But just friends?"

"Yes."

He looks over to where Tanner's dancing. "Well, that'll
make all the girls happy, anyway."

"And what about the guys? They don't care that I'm single?"

"Oh no." His expression is serious. "They all know Shaw
would kick their ass if they touched you. I'd do it just to get a rise
out of him, but I play for the other team, so I doubt he'd care."

I roll my eyes. "He wouldn't care regardless. I've dated lots
of guys and he hasn't touched any of them."

Lots is a stretch, but my point stands.

"Well, in that case, do you want to dance?"

I place my hand in his and let him pull me to my feet.

When we get close, Tanner spots me and smiles. We all
dance for several more songs before taking a break. A bunch of
us jump into the water to cool off. I grab on to Tanner's back
to stay afloat while he sits on a noodle.

The number of times people make some offhanded
comment assuming we're together becomes laughable. I guess
since everyone at Valley knows, I forgot how interesting
people find it that we're as close as we are but not dating.

"He's like my brother," I insist, although as soon as I say
the words, that feels weird too.

"I've seen Shaw with Tara. He isn't like that." Jonah raises
his brows and smirks at Tanner.

"You're telling me that you two have never hooked up?"
Ollie asks.

"We kissed once years ago," I say as if it meant nothing. Another thing on the list of my self-imposed rules around my best friend—don't mention that kiss. But the truth is, we kissed and we've still managed to be friends after.

I think I've pacified them until Ollie says. "Show me. Kiss her, Shaw."

He laughs but soon all twenty or so people in the water are chanting for us to kiss.

Kiss. Kiss. Kiss.

Tanner glances to me with an apologetic expression.

"Fuck off y'all," he says. "We don't have to prove anything."

They keep chanting.

"Sorry." His voice is low so that only I can hear. "Ignore them."

"It's fine. We've done it before. It's no big deal, right?"

He still looks hesitant, so I make the move. Pulling his head to mine, I press my lips to his.

It's two long seconds that my mouth is on his before he kisses me back. Slowly at first, but then his tongue is demanding entrance. My heart hammers in my chest and I tighten my hold around his neck and press my body underwater closer to his.

I kiss him to prove that we're just friends. That just because society has this idea about guys and girls not being able to be friends, we don't have to fit into that mold. What we are is something so much more. Something that can't be defined, but definitely doesn't mean what they think it does.

With the taste of alcohol and lake water on our lips and cheers among the group all around us, I realize the only thing that I've proved is that I was so very, very wrong.

Chapter Nine

TANNER

There are some things men do out of pure self-preservation. We pretend we're as handsome as Henry Cavill and as funny as Trevor Noah, we joke about how our balls are gonna sag one day (so we don't have to think about it happening for real), and we absolutely don't allow ourselves to picture having sex with our best friend.

As Sydney finally pulls back from a kiss that's left me speechless, my self-preservation dies a hard, blue death. *At least they're still hanging where they should and not down at my knees.*

My best friend still has one arm wrapped around my neck and holds the other over her head in victory. "See?"

Yeah, see? Uhhh, wait, what?

Jonah shakes his head. "Damn. I got turned on just watching that kiss."

I steel my expression when Sydney looks back to me.

"Sorry about that. You know me, I can never back down from a dare or competition." Her voice is tight and brittle. Awkwardness fills the space between us.

"I'm not sure kissing me was the best recourse this time," I say with tease in my tone. "I'm so good-looking it was bound to look hot to them even if you and I both know it was just a kiss."

My words do the trick of chasing away the weirdness and Sydney smiles and rolls her eyes. "You made that kiss look hot? Please, it was all me."

Fuck yeah, it was.

We get back on the boat. The mood is light and everyone else is ready to keep partying. I only had the one beer hours ago because I'm driving the boat back, but even if I could get wasted, I'm not feeling it anymore. I'm staying sober enough to be the responsible one in the friendship.

Maybe a part of me has always known my feelings for Sydney went beyond friends, but I've managed with the simple fact that she didn't feel the same. And I'd do anything to be in her life, even pretend I don't think she's the hottest girl on the planet.

But Sydney seems to have lost some of her excitement for partying too. She's reserved and quiet, two things very un-Sydney like.

"You good? We can go back any time you want."

"I am a little tired."

"What?" Jonah butts in. "It's early. And we're going to The Cove tonight."

"It's been a long day." I'm already picturing being back at my place with just Sydney and away from people who make me confront or analyze who we are to one another.

"Come on," Jonah whines.

"I'll call you later." I lift my hand and he grabs it and pulls me to him and whispers near my ear, "You're totally going back to bang, right? That kiss was on fire."

I step back without a response and wave to the rest of the people on the boat. "See you guys later."

Sydney waves her goodbye and we head down to my smaller boat. She settles back in on the same seat she sat on during the ride up while I untie us and start toward the house.

"I think I drank too much," she says on a yawn.

"Being on the water all day will take it out of you. I'm sure the alcohol didn't help."

"I just need a nap and then I'll be ready to go out tonight." She yawns again.

By the time I get us home, Sydney is passed out. I gather all the stuff before waking her.

"Babe, we're back."

Her lids are slow to open. She sits up and stretches, arms out to her sides. The movement pushes out her boobs. I glance down at my feet so I don't give away my thoughts while I lift the cooler onto the dock and then step off the boat. I help her out and we start back.

Either I'm speed walking or she's slower than normal. I pause to let her catch up.

"Sorry, I'm so tired. I can barely pick my feet up."

"Ride?"

She grins and I turn my back to her and wait for her to hop on. I carry her piggyback to the house and up the back stairs while dragging the cooler—next level multi-tasking. I leave the cooler on the deck and Sydney hops down.

The awkwardness is back now that we're in this big house all alone.

"I'm going to shower. Do you need anything?"

She fidgets and bites at the corner of her lip. "No, I think I'll shower quick too."

"Cool." Holy awkward, Batman.

In the shower, I lean a hand against the wall and drop my head to let out a long, frustrated sigh. I hate conflict and drama. Sydney and I have always been able to talk things out. Maybe I haven't been one hundred percent honest with her, but I've sacrificed to keep our friendship. That's the most important thing. Still is.

Dripping wet, I pad out of the bathroom running a towel over my chest. I dry off quickly to go find Sydney. I don't want to go to sleep before we've cleared the air. I toss the towel and grab shorts from my bag. I'm about to head to her room when I spot a Sydney-sized lump on my bed. Upon further inspection, she's passed out cold.

I climb into bed beside her. Her long, wet hair has soaked both pillows. Such a pain in the ass. The smile on my face and the lightness in my chest reminds me I don't mind her brand of pain. It's a relief to have her here and to know that despite the weirdness today, she still wants to be near me.

It's dark out when I wake up. Low music filters from somewhere in the house and Sydney sings along. I find her in the kitchen cooking grilled cheese sandwiches.

"Hey," she says. "You're up. Hungry?"

"Yeah, starved actually."

She points a spatula toward a plate with two sandwiches on it, both cut diagonally.

I take a seat at the counter and watch as she finishes her food and puts it on a plate. I'm working out how to best broach the topic of what I will now forever think of as the greatest kiss of my life. She gets there first.

"About today," she starts as she takes a seat next to me. "I'm really sorry. I should not have put you in that position. I'd been drinking, not that it's an excuse, and I guess I just really wanted to prove to everyone that what we have is real. You're my best friend, Tanner. I never want to do anything to put that in jeopardy."

I'm waiting for an opening to speak, but she just keeps going. "You just got out of a relationship and I think I've been feeling a little lonely and jumped at any opportunity for a spark with someone, even you. Plus, we had our window years ago. If anything was going to happen, that was the time. Not now when we have this great friendship."

Finally, she goes quiet and takes a deep breath. She said a lot and I'm still wrapping my brain around some of it, but the most important thing I say without hesitation, "You're my best friend too. Nothing will ever change that."

"Promise?" She looks more vulnerable than I've ever seen her, and I realize just how much I mean to her, too.

I take her hand in mine and gently squeeze her long, delicate fingers. "I promise. I'm not going anywhere."

The relief she feels is evident in the relaxing of her shoulders. Conversation is still stilted, though, as we eat and clean up the kitchen together.

I'm scanning texts from Jonah and Ollie about their plans for the night while she starts the dishwasher.

"Do you feel like going out tonight?" I ask.

"Am I totally boring if I say no?"

"Not at all. We've got an entire month. Movie night?"

Her eyes light up. "Yes, that sounds perfect."

I let Sydney run the remote and pick what we watch. That nap earlier only served to make me more tired, and I have a sneaking suspicion I'm going to pass out five minutes in. She picks one of the *Mission Impossible* films—they're all basically the same—and we lay together on the couch.

Now that I've had time to think about what she said earlier, there's one piece that keeps bothering me. She said, we had our window. I don't deny that part, but it's the way she said it, like it wasn't what she wanted.

That isn't how I remember it. I kissed her and she shut it down. And, yeah, I thought something would happen eventually but the more we hung out the closer we became and I thought it was a mutual decision that neither of us wanted to risk our friendship for more. To think that we might have hooked up and then never spoke again, seriously makes me feel sick even now.

"Hey." We're laying at opposite ends of the couch and I nudge her elbow with my foot. "Remember our first kiss?"

She looks surprised I brought it up at first but then smiles. "Yeah, of course. We were in the pool at The White House."

"What is it with us and water?"

We both laugh, and then it's quiet, except for the suspenseful background music of the movie.

"What about it?" she asks.

"I was thinking back to that night and those first few weeks we hung out. I wanted to kiss you again so bad, but I was scared of freaking you out or pressuring you. You intimidated the hell out of me."

"No way." Her brown eyes stare back intensely.

"Yes way. I figured it was obvious."

"Not to me. I thought I turned you off with my five-date thing."

"What five-date thing?"

"My five-date rule," she says again like that's supposed to

mean something to me. "I had a rule about not hooking up with anyone before five dates. Actually the rule died after you."

"It did? Why did it start?"

"Remember the guy, Will, that I told you about?"

"The dickwad who ghosted you?"

She nods. "After him, I was determined to make sure I didn't let anyone else take advantage of me like that, so I told you I had a five-date rule to keep myself from sleeping with you and then being hurt when you never called me again."

"I wouldn't have done that."

"Which is why I gave up on the rule. It obviously didn't work."

"Well, it kept us from sleeping together."

"The idea was that I would get to know a person before I jumped into bed with them. You and I hung out a ton, way more than five dates. I came over in my cutest dresses to play video games for crying out loud. I figured you thought I was too high maintenance or crazy."

"I completely forgot about the five-date rule. I was waiting for you to give me the go-ahead that you were ready and then it felt like the moment had passed." Five dates or five hundred, if I'd known that was what was stopping her, I'd have given them to her to prove how much I wanted her.

"Strange to think about how it might have been different if I'd kept my mouth shut that night."

"Well, I would have tried to get you naked and probably made you feel like I was another Will, so it was probably for the best."

"Yeah, I guess so."

"Even knowing I potentially missed out on seeing you naked..." Jesus, just thinking about having sex with her, my voice goes gruff and my dick stiffens. "I think I got a pretty good deal having you as a best friend instead."

"Do you think it's possible we would have hooked up and still been friends like we are now?"

I really wish the answer to that was yes. It'd make entertaining the idea of doing something about it now to make up for two years ago a lot easier. "Probably not, but part of me wishes we had anyway."

Her grin lights up the room. "Same. I think it would have been good."

My face feels warm. Actually my whole body does, straight down to my groin. "No doubt about that, babe."

No freaking doubt.

Chapter Ten

SYDNEY

Over the next week, Tanner and I spend most of our days on the water and our nights at home watching movies.

In the days since I kissed him, things have slowly gone back to normal. That kiss. Holy shit, that kiss. My body tingles just thinking about it. Every time I look at him now, I can practically feel his lips on mine.

Our first kiss was fun and exciting and sure it was sexy, but our second kiss was full of two years of frustration. We could have powered a city with the sparks from that kiss.

And it was good to finally talk about the kiss two years ago. Everything is out in the open now and we can go back to being just friends. I convince myself of that several times a day, but when I walk out onto the deck where Tanner is kicked back staring at the water—my good intentions speed by with the boats.

I like him. No, I love him. Some of those feelings are purely because he's my best friend and favorite person, but not all of them. If my emotions were a pie chart, there's a little sliver of the pie that's uncategorized and confusing the shit out of me.

I'm busy gawking at my handsome best friend, head spinning around those feelings, when Tanner turns to face me. His lips part into a big smile. "Hey."

I take a seat beside him but then stand again. Sitting still is not in the cards today. I have too many thoughts in my head to be idle. "I think I'm going to go for a run."

His feet come off the railing and he stands. "That sounds good, actually. Let me put on my shoes."

We take off at a jog on the path. It's hot and humid and whose idea was this anyway? Truth be told, when I said I was going for a run I meant alone, and that I'd run until I was out of sight and then walk.

"Datson is coming tomorrow." Tanner keeps at my slower pace. "His parents don't live too far from here, so he's driving up for the night."

"Oh yeah? Do I need to make myself scarce for a big, blowout party?"

He grins and gives me a weird look. Probably because he's never, not once, hung out with a friend or had a party that didn't include me.

"Thought we could take him out on the boat and Jonah mentioned having a party at his place."

"Sounds good."

I lengthen my stride and push us a little harder. Thanks to volleyball, I'm in good shape and my competitive spirit makes me want to impress Tanner even though I know he's probably only giving seventy-five percent.

We run in silence for a half hour. Our breathing syncs, as do our footsteps. The path curves along the water's edge and we come to a more secluded area.

"Does this go all the way around back to your place?"

"Eventually, probably. I've never tested it. It's got to be seven or eight miles."

I stop and my chest lifts and falls as I suck in deep breaths. "Fuck that."

Tanner stops and comes back with a smirk on his face. "You're cute when you cuss."

"Shut it." I start back at a jog in the opposite direction. I don't hear Tanner's steps behind me and glance over my shoulder. "Are you coming?"

He's kicked off his socks and shoes and is pulling his shorts down, giving me a glimpse of his black boxer briefs.

"What are you doing?"

"Cooling off. It's about a thousand degrees out here. Who goes for a run in this heat?"

"You didn't have to come." Sweat drips down my neck.

"But I did and now I want to swim for a few minutes." He inches his boxer briefs down and then pauses. "Better look away unless you want to see my very white ass."

Rolling my eyes, I give him my back. "Since when are you so modest?"

"I'm not, but thought I'd give you the chance to choose whether or not you looked. All right. I'm going in."

I turn in time to see a flash of his backside as he jumps in, holding a hand over his dick. He goes under and comes back up with a smile and runs a hand over his face and pushes his hair out of his eyes.

"I am not skinny dipping with you."

"Your loss." He makes a big show of tilting back and floating in the water. Relaxed and enjoying himself far too much.

He's not even looking at me, but as soon as I toe off the first shoe, he grins all too knowingly.

I strip down to my sports bra and then hesitate with my shorts, finally saying screw it and adding them to my pile of clothes. While it isn't a bathing suit, my bra and underwear cover more than some of my bikinis. I walk out onto the small dock and Tanner swims closer.

A few boats dot the water in the distance, but other than that, there's no one around. I jump in, the cold jolting me at first.

"Oh, that does feel nice."

"Told you."

Closing my eyes, I lay back and float beside him. The sun is still hot, but the chill of the water makes it perfect.

"Sometimes, I guess, you have good ideas."

"Sometimes?" A spray of water hits my face.

Keeping my eyes closed, I splash in the general direction of him. "I need a lake house. It's my new life goal."

"I hear that. Maybe when my parents croak, they'll leave me theirs."

I snort laugh. "Your life goal is dependent on the two people who love you most in the world dying?"

"Don't knock my dreams." He hums deep in his throat. "Last summer."

"Yeah, I've been thinking about that too."

"About what you're going to do without me?"

"We've spent summers apart before," I remind him.

"Yeah, I know, but what if you end up on one side of the world and I'm on the other?"

"We'll see each other when we can. Plus, we can text and video chat."

"Let's make a pact."

Opening my eyes, I smile at him. "A pact? What are you, twelve?"

He splashes water at me again.

"Can we talk about this on the way back? My legs are jelly, and if we keep treading water, you're going to have to carry me back to the house."

His gaze drops below my face but from the neck down I'm below the water, so his scan of my body is thwarted. It gives me a small thrill that he attempted to check me out anyway.

"I'm enjoying this. Grab on."

I wrap my arms around his chest from behind and without thinking, circle his waist with my legs. It isn't until my foot brushes against his dick that I realize my mistake and quickly bring my legs back behind him. Bare ass I can handle... bare dick... big nope.

"Try not to kick me in the balls." He chuckles.

If he's felt uncomfortable since our kiss, he hasn't shown it. I desperately wish I could go back to when I wasn't so aware of him. They were simpler times.

But I *am* all too aware of him. His back, for example. The man has back muscles that are hard and flex in front of me. And his chest and abs are defined. Not too bulky, but it's obvious that he's got more than a skinny-guy six-pack. I'm not even going to mention his butt. Captain America has America's ass? Please. Tanner wins that contest every day of the week. His aforementioned lack of modesty has given me plenty of glimpses over the years.

Yeah, Tanner's ridiculously hot. I've always known all of these things. I didn't suddenly gain the ability to see. That kiss just made me less objective about it. Hot is just hot, but the chemistry I felt kissing him can't be as easily dismissed. Long ago before I knew how awesome he was, maybe. Definitely

not now. Especially when I know he feels the same way
—or did.

"Okay, so back to my genius idea," he says.

I don't have to look at him to know he has an excited grin
on his face. Tanner doesn't always show his emotions on his
face, but right now as I glance to confirm my suspicion, he's
easy to read with a big smile that stretches ear to ear.

"We promise to meet up here every summer. No matter
what."

"O-kay."

"You agreed to that way faster than I expected. Damn, I'm
good." He twists his head around so our faces are close enough
that I could kiss him by barely moving. "You mean it?"

"I think I can manage that." Even as I say it, my stomach
dips at the thought of only seeing him once a year. Yeah, I'm
sure we'll stay friends but eventually he'll get a serious girlfriend and get married and we'll drift apart. I think he's far
more likely to back out on our deal than I am.

Unlike me, Tanner's had some semi-serious relationships
over the years. None of the girls were even remotely good
enough for him, but I liked them well enough.

"Have you heard from Amelia?"

"Nah, that's definitely over."

"I'm sorry. I know how much you cared about her."

His shoulders shrug. "Yeah, I guess. I mean I did, of course
I did, but I feel fine about it. She isn't someone I could see
myself with long-term."

"That's because you know as soon as you get back to Valley,
you'll have your pick of girls again. Boys have it so freaking
easy."

"What, like you couldn't have any guy you wanted? I can't
tell you the number of times I've almost maimed someone in

the locker room for speaking their unfiltered thoughts about you."

"Really?"

He chuckles at my excitement. "Really."

"Hmm. Maybe you can hook me up with one of them."

His blue eyes bore into me as if he's checking to see if I'm serious. "No."

"Why not?"

"They aren't good enough for you. College guys are trash."

"Oh, please. Come on, there has to be someone you like well enough to set me up with? It's been months since I dated anyone. I think I'm ready."

He studies my face for a second as if to gauge my sincerity. "All right. I will think about it, but no ballplayers. It'd be too weird."

I let go of him and swim toward shore. "Come on. I need a few minutes to dry off."

"Yeah, I suppose I should get back. I told Jonah I'd go over this afternoon and work out with him."

"At his house?"

"He's got a gym in his garage. Just a half-rack and some weights. Enough for us to get in some workouts over the summer."

I hop out first and walk toward my clothes. Tanner follows behind me, cupping himself until he reaches his boxers. I take a seat in the grass to dry off before getting dressed. Once he has on his boxers, he joins me.

The early afternoon sun feels like it's zapping the water from my skin in seconds. I already want to jump back in. "Maybe I'll take a nap when we get back."

He chuckles. "You just woke up."

"It's summer vacation."

"Come with me. Jonah has a great pool. You can swim or you can watch us work out." He winks.

When Tanner said Jonah had a great pool, he wasn't lying. It's huge and has its own lazy river. The house is just as ridiculous which makes me curious as to what it is Jonah's family does to own a place like this.

We all sit out back next to the pool for a while before Jonah and Tanner decide it's time to get their workout in.

"You good?" Tanner asks me.

"Oh yeah," I say, pulling my T-shirt over my head. "I'll be just fine."

Jonah tilts his head toward the house. "There's beer, wine, and some other drinks in the kitchen. Help yourself."

They disappear inside and I finish undressing and then slather my body in sunscreen, don my sunglasses, and grab one of the rafts stacked up beside the pool. As I'm slipping into the water, music filters out from speakers around the pool. Yep, a lake house just like this is definitely a life goal.

I float around the pool for who knows how long. I'm in that happy state where my brain is turned off and I only exist in bliss and peace. My phone rings and breaks the moment, snapping me back to reality. I consider letting it go, but I've already been knocked out of my pool bliss, so I climb out and grab it.

"Hey," I say, answering with a smile that Emily can't see but I'm sure comes across in my voice.

"Hey, I was just about to hang up. You sound way happier than I expected for a girl back in her hometown, or have you started drinking already this afternoon? No judgment. I know how much you hate it there."

"Actually, I had a change of plans and I'm at the lake with Tanner."

"Oh, that's awesome. You're there for the weekend?"

"For the month."

She's silent for a moment and then, "What about Amelia?"

"They broke up." It sort of annoys me that I wouldn't be allowed to be here if he had a girlfriend like I'm the evil best friend who is trying to steal Tanner away. I mean, okay, I did kiss him, but I definitely wouldn't have if he had a girlfriend.

More silence.

"We're over at one of his friend's houses today. Em, you should see this place. The house is as big as The White House but right on the lake and he's got this huge pool... I never want to leave."

"Sounds awesome. I was calling to make sure you hadn't fallen into depression and turns out you're having a better summer than me. I'm jealous."

"Why? What's going on with you? When do you leave for Disney?" Her family's summer vacation plans of going to Orlando to visit Disney World and the beach is all she's talked about for the past two months.

"Eh, that sort of fell through. My mom got shingles and all she wants to do is sit inside in front of the fan."

"Sorry." I sit beside the pool and stick my legs into the water, capturing a bit of the bliss like a contact high. "You should come visit."

"I bet Tanner would love that. He finally gets you to himself, and you still find ways to cockblock him."

I fumble for words. "I'm not... he's not... we're..."

"I was kidding, but wow, you sound guilty. Did you two

finally hook up? You bitch. I expected you to call me immediately when that happened. Tell me everything."

"You misunderstood. I only meant that he doesn't care about having me alone. Datson is coming up tomorrow, and his sister and her friends are coming later this month. We're just friends, Em." I do consider telling her about the kiss, but I think that will only add fuel to her theory that Tanner and I are inevitable.

Maybe it's part of my stubborn competitiveness, but the more people insist Tanner and I are more than friends, the more I want to prove them wrong. Sparks be damned.

Chapter Eleven

TANNER

Jonah racks the barbell and we both move to add another plate to either side before taking a quick rest between sets.

He takes a seat on the bench and wipes his forehead with a towel. "What are you guys doing tonight? Do you want to head over to The Cove?"

"That sounds good. I'll run it by Sydney."

"What's up with you two? I can't figure you out."

"We're friends, man. I've told you a million times."

"I don't buy it, and it's not because I don't think guys and girls can be friends. It's the way you talked about her all these years and then seeing you two together."

"Sydney is super competitive. You guys were basically daring her to kiss me, therefore guaranteeing that she would just to prove you wrong."

"That kiss was fucking hot. Best guy on girl soft-core porn I've ever seen, but that's not what I mean. It's when you are just sitting next to one another or standing together. There's this connection and awareness, soul-deep shit that I won't even pretend to understand, but I know isn't normal friend behavior."

"Soul-deep shit?" I ask with a chuckle.

He lays back on the bench for his next set, and I get in position to spot him. He gets five easy and I help him push out two more.

"If I had that with someone, I wouldn't be so quick to dismiss it, that's all I'm saying," he says, still breathing hard.

"I don't take it for granted for a second," I tell him honestly. "She's the best thing that's ever happened to me." I know it sounds cheesy as hell, but it's true.

He nods in understanding. "You might want to examine why that is." He holds his hands up defensively, probably at the hard look I'm giving him. "I've said my peace."

"Noted." Eager to change the subject, I ask, "You remember my friend John Datson? He came up last summer and went to The Cove with us over Memorial Day weekend. Anyway, he's coming up tomorrow."

"Datson! Yeah, love that guy. He's a good time."

I chuckle. That he is. They are a lot alike in that regard. Datson's a good guy, and definitely always up for a good time.

"I have a few friends coming up this weekend, too. A couple of very good-looking girl *friends*. And by friends I mean people I don't want to hook up with. You know, since we seem to have different definitions of the word." He winks. "I think you'll like Willow. Tall, blonde… that is your type, right?"

I flip him off. He's not wrong. That's exactly my type.

We finish up in the gym and head inside. We're both already in our swim trunks and I'm dying to get in that pool to cool off. Jonah mixes up protein smoothies for us and I stare out the window to where Sydney's floating on a yellow raft.

He brings me a strawberry smoothie and a water. He's carrying his own drink and smoothie, and we take a step outside before I stop in my tracks. "I should grab Sydney something."

Jonah chuckles. "So thoughtful. In the door of the fridge." He continues on and I go back to get another water.

The extra twenty seconds gives Jonah a chance to grab a floatie and join Sydney. I sit on the edge of the pool while I finish my drink. They're at the farthest point on the lazy river. Their voices and laughter are barely heard over the music. Jonah is complimenting her body and Sydney's laughing as he goes on and on and on and on. Your stomach and those shoulders. All right, Jonah, that's enough I want to tell him. But the smile on her face as they come into view stops me. He's not saying anything that isn't true and anything that makes her happy, makes me happy.

We stay at Jonah's house until around dark. Sydney was all about going out tonight, so we head back to shower and get ready.

For all the things Sydney and I have done together, we've never gotten ready for a party or a night out at the same place. It almost feels like a date as I sit in the living room scrolling through my phone waiting on her.

She's come out three times with different dresses to ask my opinion. Her style is short, tight, and colorful and there's absolutely no way to go wrong with that so I'm not a lot of help. Torture devices? Yes. But the good kind of torture.

"Babe, Uber's going to be here in three minutes. Are you almost—"

My words die as she steps into view.

"I'm ready. I'm ready." Thankfully she's staring down at the small purse she carries, so she doesn't see my jaw drop to the ground and hang out there while my eyes scan her from head to toe.

Tonight's torture device isn't a dress, but the amount of pain it causes remains the same. A plain white tank top is tucked into a hot pink skirt that ends waaay above her knees. It's just a step above indecent. She got some sun the last few days and her skin has this smooth and satiny look to it. I want to run my hands up her legs and see if they're really as smooth as marble. It's the sort of thing I might have joked about just a few days before, but the tightening of my jeans in the crotch area refuses to let me play it off like that.

"Tanner?" Sydney asks. Her brows knit in concern.

"Sorry, what?"

"Does this look okay?" She runs a hand along her waist. "I don't usually wear skirts because I don't like the way the band feels around my stomach and I swear somehow that tiny piece of added fabric makes my boobs look smaller, but... what do you think?"

"Skirt good. Very good. Err..." I shake my head. "I think my brain exploded. You look amazing."

Her smile says she believes me. Sydney doesn't often need or request my praise, but after seeing how happy she was when Jonah fawned over her earlier, I realize I need to be quicker to give it. A job I'm happy to do.

I stand and close the distance between us. Running my hand down her arm, because I can't freaking help myself, I breathe her in. She smells like my shampoo and body wash and fuck, why is that so hot?

"You look pretty good yourself." She places a hand on my chest. It's when she compliments me that I realize I may not have been doling out the praise, but she always has. A new shirt or even an old one that she thinks fits me well, a good hair day, little things sometimes, but she's always looked for, and been verbal about, the ways I impress her.

I'm a fucking idiot.

"Let's go show you off." I hold my arm out, and she grabs on to my bicep.

The Cove is only about five minutes by boat but by car it takes us almost thirty. The Uber pulls up to the front door and I climb out behind Sydney.

The bar is at the front of the place leaving room for tables on the back half that look out at the lake. We squeeze in and order drinks. A band is set up on one side and they're covering a Heart song. Sydney sways in place to the music.

"I know that look," I tell her, shaking my head. "I'm going to have to carry you off the dance floor tonight, aren't I?"

She grins. Yep, that's a yes.

We take our drinks and weave through the crowd. Jonah is easy to spot, especially since he's somehow commandeered three tables. They're pushed together and pitchers of beer and empty shot glasses line the surface.

"Hey!" Jonah calls out when he sees us. "Syd, I saved you a seat next to me."

She rushes off without hesitation and I take the only other seat on the opposite side by Ollie and a couple of guys I recognize from the boat yesterday.

The band continues to cover popular songs from the past thirty years which fits the mix of ages in here.

I'm half-listening to the guys and sneaking glances at Sydney across the table. She and Jonah talk and laugh. He stands and helps her to her feet.

"So, Tanner," Ollie starts, pulling my attention away from the hot, blonde otherwise known as my best friend. "Which are you going to do after college, baseball or basketball? I assume they're both scouting you."

"I'm not sure." I finish off my beer and set it on the table.

"Maybe you could do like Michael Jordan did. Play a few years of one and then switch."

Laughter slips out. "Even Jordan didn't pull that off."

The truth is, I haven't decided. I don't want to give up either. Each professional organization has pros and cons and the lifestyle of both will be brutal. Tara's definitely right about that even if I'd never admit it to her. Still I can't imagine giving up either let alone both.

Every time I think I've made up my mind, I change it. I still have some time before I need to commit to anything, and I'm going to take all that I need to make sure I make the right decision.

Thinking about that is depressing as hell though, so I stand to get another beer from the bar. Sydney and Jonah are on the dance floor, front and center.

With a fresh beer, I lean a hip against the bar and watch them. Jonah holds on to Sydney's hands and lifts them so that she can twirl. Seeing two people from different parts of my world hitting it off so well gives some sort of balance to my life. Sydney and I are so much alike, I don't expect there's anyone in my life she wouldn't get along with.

I head back to the table and fall back into conversation with Ollie. He's telling me about his part-time job at the golf course when long arms wrap around my neck from behind. Sydney's hair falls over my shoulder before she leans down so we're cheek to cheek. She still smells like my bodywash but now it's intertwined with sweat and alcohol. That should turn me off, but it doesn't.

"Did they kick you off the floor already?"

"Quick hydration break."

I hand her the diet and Malibu I got for her at the bar.

"Oh you're a prince." She takes it and moves to sit on my lap facing Ollie.

"What happened to Jonah?" he asks her.

"He's waiting for the band to break so he can talk to the lead singer."

We all turn to get a look at Jonah standing at the bar with his back against the hard wood. Even from here I can tell his gaze is on the tall, lanky guy crooning into the microphone.

"Never happen." Ollie chuckles. "He's been working up the courage for weeks now. Every time Jonah comes up with one excuse or another why he didn't get a chance."

"I didn't take him for the shy type." Sydney cranes her neck farther to watch the two of them. "We should help."

Ollie groans. I manage to keep my initial reaction to myself.

"How exactly would we help?" I ask and then regret that question immediately when Sydney goes into scheming mode.

"What if, you talked to him first and then you could introduce them?"

"Why me?"

"Because I'm not his type." She waves a hand in front of her boobs.

Ollie laughs.

I kick his chair. "Why don't you do it?"

"Oh no, you're much prettier than I am. Our best shot is sending in the ringer."

He and Sydney both stare at me expectantly.

"No. No way. It's a terrible plan."

Sydney looks at me with those big, brown eyes. "What if that cute singer is Jonah's soul mate and he never meets him because he was too shy? Can you really live with that guilt?"

Chapter Twelve

SYDNEY

"What is he doing?" Jonah asks as Tanner approaches the stage where the band is packing up.

We gave Jonah until the end of the set to make a move, but as Ollie predicted, he only stared at the handsome lead singer.

"He's being your wingman," I tell him with a little poke in the chest.

Jonah's brows shoot up under the dark red hair falling onto his forehead. Then he laughs. "Well, that's ironic. The only guy in this place that's more chickenshit than me is helping me out. *Fuck*." He pushes off the bar and his jaw flexes. "All right." He strides toward them.

"What just happened?" I ask Ollie on my other side.

"Our plan worked." He shrugs.

Jonah squeezes Tanner's shoulder and says something that makes the singer laugh. Tanner opens his stance, and the three of them talk back and forth for a few minutes before the suspense is killing me, and I go in.

Tanner glances up as I get near and smiles. He wraps an arm around my waist and pulls me to his side. I love when he claims me like this, even if it's only meant to be a friendly gesture. Maybe it should annoy me because it undoubtedly scares men away, but I really don't care.

"Was the last song an original?" Jonah is asking the singer. "I've never heard it before."

"Yeah." He shoves his hands in the front of his jeans pockets. Without a microphone, he looks a lot shier than he did. He's got a nice, friendly smile. I can see why Jonah's into him. "Did it suck?"

"What? No way. You should play more originals. It was bomb." Jonah tilts his head toward the bar. "Can I buy you a drink?"

"I should help the guys load up first. Will you be around for a while?"

After making plans to meet up with us, hottie singer whose name I find out is Richard, goes back to his band, and Jonah wears the largest grin I've ever seen as we go back to the table.

"Nice work," Tanner tells him. "Knew you had it in you. You just needed a little competition."

"Please. Even if you were gay, you are so not his type."

"I want to be offended by that, but I'm going to let it go because I'm happy for you." Tanner lifts his glass. "Cheers, buddy."

The mood is light, and the drinks seem to be drained faster the later it gets. Richard and one of his bandmates join us. Jonah may have been too shy to approach the handsome guy he's had his eye on, but he's found his confidence now as he rests an arm around his chair and chats him up.

"They're cute," I tell Tanner. Everyone around us is in conversation making it loud so we have to lean in close. He reaches over and pulls my chair next to his and then rests his hand on my thigh.

"What's that? Did you say I'm cute?"

"I said *they're* cute." I glance to Jonah and Richard. "Way to make it about you."

"Last summer he was dating someone, so I've never seen his game or lack thereof before." His long fingers are still on my leg radiating heat through my skin to my core.

"What about you?" I ask, trying to ignore the way my body feels at his touch. "Do you hook up at the lake?"

His face tells me the answer even before he does. "Sometimes. It's hard to take anything too seriously knowing I'm going back to Valley in a few weeks. It's like a really long spring break. Nobody is looking for a relationship at the lake."

I snort. "More lake rules by Tanner?"

"Something like that." His gaze falls to his hand on my leg as if he's suddenly realized he's touching me, and he removes it to grab his beer on the table. "Don't act like you haven't had your summer flings. What about that guy you met in Japan?"

"It was Italy, and his name was Sebastian."

He shrugs as if the place as well as the guy is inconsequential. He's mostly right. Although I had hoped things with the cute volleyball player I met in Italy last summer while playing in the world championship volleyball tournament would go beyond the month we were in the same country, but it was just too hard with the distance.

"You ready? If we don't get an Uber soon, then we'll be sitting outside after closing."

I nod my agreement and we say bye to everyone and get in our ride back to his place. He sits in the middle of the back seat so we're side by side.

I'm staring at the lake at night and the dot of lights as we pass by when Tanner nudges me with his elbow. "You're staring out that window awfully hard. What are you thinking about?"

I put my head on his shoulder. "I was thinking about what you said earlier. How you can't picture something more with a fling or hookup you meet during the summer. The thing is, I think some people—mostly girls it seems—hope beyond reason that a summer fling will turn into more. I've rarely hooked up with anyone that I couldn't see a future with. I just think it's interesting. The girls you hooked up with were probably hoping you were going to fall for them and want more."

"I am always honest about my intentions. I never promise a girl I'm going to call and then don't."

"I know, but that doesn't mean they didn't hope you'd change your mind."

"I don't think I've seen a future with any of the girls I've dated in the past two years. How sad is that?"

"Really? Why did you date them then?" I'd always wondered why Tanner had chosen the girls he did. From Amelia to the one before... I never found any real common thread to figure out what it was that made a guy like him settle down.

"I liked them, and I wanted to spend more time together. And with Amelia there were times when I could picture us together after college, but never like..." He pulls back and shakes his head. "It doesn't matter."

"Tell me."

He hesitates before saying, "The only person I've ever really been able to picture in my life forever is you."

My heart hammers in my chest and blood pounds in my ears.

"When I see my life in five years or fifty—I see it with you."

"With me as your best friend or...?"

The car pulls up at Tanner's and we climb out. I walk numbly behind him. Neither of us speaks until we're inside.

"Water?" he asks, grabbing two from the fridge.

I take one, kick off my shoes, and we go sit outside on the deck.

It's late. The moon is high in the sky and the lake is quiet. Tanner sits and then pulls me onto his lap. We've sat like this a million times. We've always been comfortable in our affection. Still, this feels different.

I'm deciding whether or not I should push for an answer to my question from the car when he starts talking again.

"I've gone over it a million different times. Wondering what would happen if I kissed you. I can't tell you how many times I've woke up with the most vivid sex dreams recreating that first night together."

"And?" My voice wavers. I'm so nervous. I'm never nervous around Tanner.

"All I know is that I want everything to be exactly the same."

My heart drops. I didn't realize how much I was hoping he wanted more until now. Then his hand lifts my chin up and slides down so he's caressing my neck. "Except I want to own your body like you own my heart."

He's still, blue eyes darkening and waiting for a response. For the second time, I make the move. This time, though, he's in control from the second my lips land on his. Tanner makes a gruff noise deep in his throat. His tongue sweeps into my mouth and the hand at my neck holds me in place as he kisses me deeply and passionately.

An ache, so deep and constant I'm not sure it can ever be soothed, throbs inside of me. I shift so that I'm straddling him. My skirt inches up on my thighs leaving nothing but the lacy material of my panties to rub against his jeans. We both groan and our kisses become frenzied and manic. I might be on top, but he has total command.

I've always loved Tanner's hands, but never more than when they're holding me in place. One at my neck, the other at my waist, his touch is gentle enough not to hurt but strong enough to distinguish this from the millions of other touches we've shared before now.

I grind into his hard erection. His hips roll underneath me, and my head falls back. He leaves hot, warm open-mouth kisses along my collarbone and neck.

He mumbles something but the words are lost to the sensation. More. One word that sums up my current existence. I want more—need it, now and from him.

"Babe?"

"Hmm?"

"I said, I want to take you out. Do this right."

"Dating is for getting to know one another. We already know each other every way but one. Let's get naked." I climb up higher so that I'm basically fucking him through his jeans and push my breasts into his face.

His big hands come to my waist and hold me still. His dick twitches between us and I can see the knit of frustration on his face as he holds back. "I want a do-over. All the things I should have done the first time. Real dates where you dress up for me and I tell you how beautiful you are. I want to woo the fuck out of you." He lifts me off his crotch and sets me on a less bulge-y and far less fun part of his lap.

"Woo me while you fuck me."

He smiles that cocky smirk that tells me he's made up his mind no matter how much his body tells me otherwise. "That too, but first, I owe you five dates."

Chapter Thirteen

TANNER

I totally forgot about Datson coming up today when I decided to cockblock myself and take sex off the table until after I've taken Sydney on five dates. I woke up to my buddy pounding on the front door at noon ready to get out on the lake which puts a wrench in my plan for date number one.

Sleep was fitful and the blue balls I went to bed with were super distracting, so I planned out all five dates. They're epic. One plus of dating Sydney now instead of two years ago is how much more I know about her.

My dick aches to finally get inside of my best friend, but I meant what I told her... I want to do it right. Not many people get a do-over so I'm going to guess a triple-over is even rarer. I'm not going to need a third try though. I'm getting it right this time.

I can hear the shower going in Sydney's bathroom as Datson and I pack the cooler.

"Jonah's having a party tonight and Ollie's down this year too." I toss in a half-empty bottle of Malibu and a couple of cans of Coke.

"I'm so stoked to be here. Two weeks at home sweating my ass off working on the farm with my dad and brothers and I'm ready for school to start."

"Did you tell them you're not planning to work there after graduation?"

"Nah, not yet. I don't want to listen to them lecture me for the rest of the summer about letting down the family." He rolls his eyes.

The Datson family owns a farm not far from here and despite his brothers all wanting to stay and help run it, my buddy still feels pressure to go back after graduation. I think if he knew what he wanted to do instead, his family would be more understanding. All he does seem to know is it isn't farming.

I'm hardly one to talk since I'm struggling to make a decision about my own future, but I give him the advice everyone's been giving me.

"Do whatever feels right for you. It's your life." People who say that have never had any pressure from their family or coaches.

With a sigh, I give him *my* best advice—no bullshit. "Just be honest and tell them you want a chance to pursue other things. It isn't like the farm is going anywhere if you change your mind."

He mumbles his acknowledgment but in a way that I very much doubt he's going to act on my words.

The cooler is packed and I let the lid fall closed.

"All right, let's do it." He claps his hands.

I glance toward Sydney's room. The shower's not running anymore, but my girl hasn't come out.

"Let me just go check to see if Sydney's coming."

"Yeah, sure. I think I'll start down." He picks up the cooler and heads out the back door.

The door to the spare bedroom is ajar, but I knock and call out, "Babe?"

"Back here." Her voice carries from the small attached bathroom.

She's leaned over, her hair falling over her face as she finger-combs it and then flips the long, blonde mane back and stands straight. The way girls get ready is strange.

"Datson's chomping at the bit to get out on the lake. Are you ready?"

"Go ahead. I'm going into town. Coach found a physical therapist here for me to check in with, and I want to see if I can get a yoga mat and some bands for here."

I hadn't noticed before, but she's not dressed for a day on the lake. I slide a hand over her waist. The thin, cotton material of the bright yellow dress isn't as soft as her skin, but it's probably good I have a barrier right now.

Being able to touch her like this still trips me out a little. "Is it crazy that I'm thinking a day shopping sounds better than the lake right now?"

Her sweet laughter echoes in the small space, and she steps closer and wraps her arms around my neck. "You'd be bored out of your mind in the first five minutes. I know how you are with shopping."

Bored while with her? Doubtful.

"You'll come with us to Jonah's tonight, right?"

"Yeah. I'll be back later this afternoon."

"Keys to the Firebird are on the kitchen counter," I say like I'm leaving but don't move.

"Thanks. Have fun with Datson."

Still, neither of us moves. I bury my nose in the crook of her neck and breathe her in.

"I planned out our first date."

"Yeah?" I can hear the smile in her voice. "What are we doing?"

"You, your favorite dress, and me trying to keep my jaw off the table." I work my way up her neck and jaw, kissing every inch.

More of that sweet laughter slips into my mouth when her lips press against mine. "I can't wait. Gives me a good excuse to find a new favorite dress, too."

All I want to do is stay with her, take her out now, but I've waited this long. Another day or two won't kill me. I don't think anyway. I should Google the health risks of extended blue balls, just in case.

I kiss her harder to make sure she knows that just because I didn't pull her into my bed immediately last night like I very much wanted to, I want her in a way that goes so far beyond what we've shared before. This is new territory and I need her to feel the difference so there's no mistaking my intention. Things can never go back to how they were. That scares the shit out of me, but it feels too good and right to worry much.

"I better go."

"Have fun," she singsongs.

Datson and I spend the first hour out on the lake just driving around. I can see my buddy relaxing more with every passing minute. He turns the black cap covering his hair backward and takes off his T-shirt.

"Now you look like a real farmer." I point to his tan lines and then grab the sunscreen from a cabinet and hold it up.

"Nah, I'm hoping to even it out a little today." He digs around in the cooler and gets us each an ice-cold beer. I put mine in a koozie and kick back in the captain's seat. We've reached a quiet section of the lake, the same spot I brought Sydney on her first day. It's my favorite part of the nearly two-thousand-acre lake. Don't get me wrong, party cove is awesome, but this little secluded area is perfect for chilling, getting in the water, and just relaxing.

Datson and I do just that after he's finished his first beer. The water feels like it's warmed up a little over the week or maybe I'm just used to it.

He lets out a giant sigh and tilts his head up to the sky. "Now this is the life."

"It's not bad," I agree. "Is the farm really that awful?"

"It isn't the farm. I love the farm. It's my family that makes it painful. I wasn't home for two hours before my dad was cornering me to find out my graduation plans."

"What happens if you don't choose the farm?"

"They'll hire someone else."

"That's it?" I can't hide the surprise in my tone. I always assumed the ramifications must be pretty serious for as much grumbling as Datson does about it.

He stares at me blankly, like I just don't get it. "Well, what about you? Have you decided what you're going to do this fall? Baseball? Basketball? Both?"

A knot of annoyance tightens in my chest. "No and I'm not going to think about it until I have to."

"What about that scout from the Dodgers? Have you heard any more from him?"

"No, and I don't think I will. He was pretty hung up on

getting me to answer which sport I was going to explore after college."

Like everyone else.

"That sucks. I'm sorry," my buddy says.

"It's fine. I'm not going to worry about it."

There's absolutely no reason to ruin my last awesome summer by worrying about real-world shit. It'll still be there, and the decision will still suck.

The corner of Datson's lips twitch and pull into a smile. He lifts his beer. "Welcome to avoidance, brother."

Jonah's boat comes into view while we're still swimming in the water enjoying our beer and talking about everything except our futures. My mind goes there anyway, even as Jonah and Ollie jump into the water and I listen to my friends shoot the shit.

Playing two sports is a lot of planning and work. I think that's part of what I love about my summers at the lake. Sure, I could stay in Valley, do camps, work that off-season hard, but this keeps me sane.

Can I handle the life of a dual sport athlete professionally? People thought I was nuts when I signed on to play two sports at the division one college level. Pick one and specialize. I've been hearing that same advice since I was a kid. I've never wavered on my decision to chuck their advice and prove I could handle both until now.

This is my last year before the draft. Final chance to make an impact. If I continue to play both, I know that I'm making it harder to be drafted by either sport. But any time I seriously consider giving one up, I feel sick to my stomach.

Jonah finishes his beer and pulls it from the koozie. "I've got a bunch of friends that should be getting in pretty soon. Do you guys want to come back with us and hang for a while?"

"Definitely," Datson answers for us and then glances to me. "We don't have anywhere to be, right?"

"Let's do it."

Back on the boat, I check my phone for any missed texts from Sydney, but she must be enjoying her afternoon by herself. My sister tried to call but she didn't leave a text or voicemail, so it can't be that important.

Datson and I follow Jonah to his place. His friends arrive as we're getting in the pool. From a raft, I wave as Jonah introduces us to Willow, Jade, and Beth.

They go inside to drop their stuff and Jonah jumps into the water. "You're welcome, all of you."

"For?" I ask.

Datson looks at me like I'm crazy. "Dude, did you see Jade?"

With a chuckle, Jonah nods to him. "I knew you'd dig her. She looks a little like that actress you're always going on and on about. Kate Bosworth or Beckinsale... one of the Kates." He nudges me with an elbow. "And Willow. Exactly your type, Shaw." He winks.

I'm quiet.

Datson laughs. "He's right. She looks a little like Amelia and that girl you dated sophomore year."

"And Sydney," Jonah points out.

"Don't get him started, man," Datson warns. "They're just friends."

"They don't kiss like friends," Ollie chirps as he hops off his raft into the water.

Datson's head swivels back and forth. "What? When? What?" He stops on me. "You and Sydney finally kissed?"

"It wasn't like that." Not then, anyway. Sydney and I didn't talk about what, if anything, we were going to tell people, so I don't give him more than that.

Luckily, I'm quickly forgotten as Willow and the other two come out in their bathing suits. Datson doesn't waste any time chatting up Jade. She does look a little like Kate Beckinsale.

Jonah practically shoves Willow at me. She seems cool, and if things were different, she's someone I would have been into, but now I just want to get back and see if Sydney has returned.

I can hardly blame Datson for looking conflicted when I tell him I need to head back a little while later, but he comes with me so we can get ready for tonight and pick up Sydney.

The house is quiet, and my car is still gone. I shoot Sydney a text to let her know we're back and hop in the shower. My shampoo and body wash now remind me of Sydney since she's been using them for the past two weeks and I've got a stupid grin on my face as I lather up and count down the minutes until I see her again.

Chapter Fourteen

SYDNEY

I'm later than I planned getting back to the house. After an hour of physical therapy and several hours of retail therapy, I decided to get my hair trimmed. That turned into a pedicure and somehow that turned into a facial. I'm polished from head to toe.

I'm excited and nervous, and okay maybe prepping a little too much. I know that tonight is supposed to be a fun night with our friends, but who says Tanner and I can't also make a date of it? If he's holding out on me for five dates, I'm ready to get them started.

Datson's laughter and deep voice filters out from the patio as I enter, followed by Tanner's—one I know well, could pick out of a crowd anywhere. A fluttering low in my belly forces me to take a deep breath and remind myself it's just any other night. There's no reason to be this nervous. I pause in the kitchen, drop my bags, return Tanner's keys where I got them, and plug my phone in to charge.

I start toward the patio as Tanner's tall and muscular body fills the doorway.

"Hey, babe. You're back." His face lights up as he steps inside. "Sydney's here," he calls over his shoulder to Datson.

"Yo, Syd!" Datson leans his chair and cranes his neck so I can see him and waves.

"Hey! Good to see you."

"You too."

"How was shopping?" Tanner's hair is still wet and curls at the nape of his neck. He's in jeans and a black T-shirt that stretches across his chest and arms.

"Good. Sorry I'm so late." Six hours apart and there's a clumsiness between us as if neither of us knows how to act.

"It's fine. We're just chilling. We ordered food. I got you a couple of things in case you didn't eat."

"If I eat, can we consider that one date down?"

Finally, the tension breaks, and he shakes his head slowly as he closes the space between us. "No chance."

"Should I get us a ride?" Datson joins us, beer in hand. He glances between us. Tanner doesn't move or answer.

"I just need to change. I can be ready in five," I say.

"Coolio." Datson moves to the kitchen and picks up the bottle of Jager. "We've got time for a shot."

Jonah's house looks even more amazing at night. Big windows inside lead to a view of the lake. Outside, twinkle lights hang everywhere, illuminating the patio and pool.

Datson is quick to blend into the horde of people outside, but Tanner and I hang near the back-patio doors.

"You look incredible." His hand makes small circles where it rests at the middle of my back.

"Thanks. You told me once you had a thing for girls in white dresses."

"I can't believe you remember that. I don't even remember saying it. Totally true though."

"Has anyone ever told you that you have very boring taste?" I ask him. My preference for bright colors aside, Tanner's wardrobe is primarily made up of shades of gray, white, and black.

"Only you." He leans in. "You light up my world."

"Oh my god, you did not just say that." My insides go squishy no matter how cheesy it sounded.

"Totally did. Not taking it back either."

"I need to find the booze in this place because I'm entirely too sober for you right now."

His laughter is easy and light. "I got you. Come on."

There's a keg set up outside and Tanner informs me there's a stash of liquor inside that we apparently walked by while I was too busy scoping out the house. He pours foamy beer into cups for each of us.

"Shaw! Shaw!" The feminine voice invades our bubble and I turn to see a tall, blonde girl in denim cut-offs and a white bikini top jogging toward us. Her cheeks are flushed and her large, blue eyes wide with excitement when she reaches us. "Hey, you made it." Her friendly smile pulls higher when her gaze slides to me. "Hey there!"

"Willow, this is Sydney." Tanner inches closer to me. "Willow goes to college with Jonah."

"Nice to meet you," I say.

"Same." She grabs a hold of Tanner's wrist. "We need you for badminton."

"Badminton?" I ask quietly as she pulls him behind her. I

follow them to the opposite side of the yard where, sure enough, a badminton game is going on.

Willow jogs off to one side and picks up a racket on the ground. "We've got Shaw."

"Teams will be uneven," someone calls.

"It's fine. I'm good." Tanner holds up a hand and stays on the sideline beside me.

Irrational jealousy and a competitive spirit that often gets me in over my head (see kissing my best friend) makes me speak up. "Not if I play on the other team."

Tanner chuckles, which just makes me more determined.

"Afraid I'll show you up?" I bat my lashes. "How about a little wager?"

Rackets are thrust in our hands and I spin it around getting a feel for it. Have I ever played badminton before? Not that I can remember. But determination and athleticism I have, so how hard could it be?

"A wager, huh? All right. Let's hear it." Tanner's amusement is clear on his face.

"If I win—"

"Your team, you mean? If your *team* wins."

"Yeah, yeah. If my team wins, then this counts as a date."

"You're that eager to get me naked, huh?" he asks with a cocky smirk and then straightens. "Fuck, you wanting me so bad is hot."

"Yes, and your disinterest is a real lady boner killer." I take off my heels. The grass under my toes is cool.

Using the racket in his hand, Tanner tips my chin up and closes the step between us. "If your team wins, then we count this as a date, but if my team wins, you let me take you out on a real date tomorrow night after Datson leaves."

"You're wagering with something I'd say yes to anyway. Why?"

"It's what I want. Besides, beating you is victory enough for me." He winks and walks away toward the other side.

It's four against four. I'm placed in the back with a tall, lanky guy wearing a sweatband around his forehead who introduces himself as Biff. He looks like he's taking this seriously, so that's good for my team, I think.

Tanner's the only guy on the other team. Willow and two of her friends crowd around him like he's the king of badminton. I'm giving them all the stink eye when Willow takes the birdie back to a point on the ground marked by a cup of beer.

"First team to ten wins. Losing team does a shot for every point they lose by."

"What if we lose by a lot?" Celia, one of the girls on my team, asks.

Willow says something reassuring, but I focus my thoughts on winning. No, not just winning—total annihilation.

I smile sweetly at Tanner and get in position, or what I hope is badminton position.

Willow serves. It's low, just barely clearing the net.

"I got it," Celia calls it and waves her racket in the air. She, in fact, does not have it.

Her friend, Molly, who is also on our team, laughs.

"Shut it. I was close," Celia fires back, laughing at herself. "Let's see you do better."

No problem. Down by one. We got this.

Willow serves again with a similar result, though this time Celia doesn't call out, she still goes for it and puts the birdie in the net.

"Sorry," she chirps with a nervous giggle. "Sports are so not my thing."

"We could switch places if you want," I offer.

For the love of shuttlecock, say yes. I do not want to have to mow her down to take a swipe at the next serve.

"Oh, uh, sure." She's hesitant, but at her words, I step forward with a big smile and take her spot.

"Are you guys ready?" Willow asks, a note of pity in her voice that makes me grit my teeth.

"Ready."

Tanner's across from me on the other side of the net. "Just a game, babe. You get to go out with me either way."

"Uh-huh, yeah, yeah." I train my focus on Willow. "We've got this."

The only thing I hate more than losing is not being able to do anything to stop it. Willow knows exactly what she's doing or is the luckiest server in all of badminton. Now that I've moved up, her serves go longer so they're still in Celia's area to return.

When we're down five to zero, I take matters into my own hands.

"I've got it." I jog backward relieved to finally get a turn in the action, but I hit the birdie with the edge of the racket and it goes out of bounds.

"Oh," Willow groans. "I thought you guys had that one." She picks up the birdie and walks it back to serve for a seventh go.

I turn to my team. "Has anyone played before? Ideas? Tips?"

Biff nods. "I have. You've gotta hit the shuttlecock right on the cork."

Obvious? Yes, but at least he's offering up something.

"Okay, you play in the middle. Take the serve if you can, and we'll act as your backup." I look to the girls. "Don't be afraid to go for it if the birdie, shuttlecock thingy, comes at you. Let's be aggressive and get some momentum going. I can't take ten shots."

Celia nods. "Us either."

"Let's do this, then. Yeah?" Familiar pep and enthusiasm, the same kind that helps me on the sand for volleyball, lifts my spirits and amps up the enjoyment. Being competitive isn't just about winning. It's this feeling of importance and fun—capturing a moment. Sure I'm capturing it in a win/lose mindset, but the adrenaline and the thrill is what I'll remember far beyond the outcome of a random game of badminton one summer night.

Well, adrenaline, the thrill, and beating Tanner. Winning is extra sweet when it's against him.

This time when Willow serves, another perfect shot toward Celia, we're ready for it.

"Got it," Biff calls and Celia steps out of the way as he hits the birdie and sends it up toward me. I get it over the net, Tanner sends it back with a determined glint in his eye, and Biff hits it again, landing it between Tanner and Willow.

Hands over head, I'm maybe a little too overzealous about a single point while we're still down by five. Still, it gets us the desired energy bump and the game is more interesting after that. Tanner has an easy strength and power about him that makes him good at any sport and it's no shocker that badminton is among them.

He works hard at basketball and baseball, don't get me wrong, but the guy has a natural athleticism that gives him an advantage in anything requiring his body. And I'm pretty sure that covers all physical pursuits. Here's hoping.

Mind back on the game, I admit to myself maybe I was a little too confident about my own abilities of dominating any sport with a net and a ball because Willow is real close to showing me up. I admire it about her as much as I want to slam a cock in her face.... a shuttlecock, I mean.

"Game point," Tanner says as he prepares to serve.

"Don't you have to win by two?" I ask.

His brows raise and one side of his mouth lifts. "Do you really want to take two shots instead of one?"

Ugh, no, but if they get this point then it's over. Two serves and there's at least one more opportunity to turn the tables on them.

"I'm ready to be done. I want to get in the pool," Molly says, and Celia nods her agreement.

"All right," I acquiesce.

Even before the serve, I've decided I'm going for it. I won't go down without giving it my all. Tanner's serve is high and floats right toward the middle. All four of us head to the center. I call it and block everything else out.

Calm washes over me as I position my body and stretch the racket to my right to make the play. Everything slows down. Even the music and the noise from the party fades to the background.

I can practically taste victory when another racket collides with mine and together we jam the birdie between us and it falls to the ground two feet in front of us.

"Oh, sorry, I was trying to be aggressive." Celia smiles too big considering we just lost. She shrugs. "At least it's over now and we only have to take one shot."

Chapter Fifteen

TANNER

Sydney's still bristling from the loss as I bring back fresh drinks. Feet bare, shoes discarded beside her, she sits on the edge and dips her toes into the pool.

"One Malibu and Coke." I hand her a red cup and take a seat next to her.

"Thank you," she says like she's anything but thankful.

"It's not so bad. You still get to go out with me."

"Yeah, yeah. That would be more forgivable if this wasn't all your fault."

"My fault?" I bark out a laugh at how riled up she is over badminton.

"You and your stupid handsome face attracting every chick and forcing me into stupid badminton games." She waves a hand dismissively.

"I seem to remember you offering yourself up to even the teams."

"Yes, but I had to. I saw the way Willow was looking at you."

"How's that?"

Her brown eyes lock on me. The neon lights from the pool dot her irises. "Fishing for compliments?"

"Only from you. I don't give a shit about Willow or any other girl. Not here and not at Valley. You've always been my number one. When have I ever put anyone over you? I care what you think. Only you."

A little of the fight leaves her and her mouth softens. "I know. It doesn't mean I don't like proving that I'm better for you to anyone that tries to get your attention. I've waited two years for this. I don't want anyone to get in the way. And I don't want to wait. I don't need five dates. I did then, but not now."

"Maybe I do. I want to show you that I'm serious about doing things right this time around. I fucked it up two years ago and I really hate fucking up. I want to give you an epic love story. You deserve that."

"Epic love story?" Her grin is as wide as her face. "You're so cheesy."

"You haven't seen the half of it, babe." I get to my feet and hold out my hand. "Come on, let's enjoy the party."

Jonah is standing in a circle with two other guys, one I recognize by face but don't know his name. The guy to his right, though, I remember both face and name.

"Hey, Richard. Good to see you again," I say.

"You too, Shaw." He looks to Sydney. "See you've got your girl with you again tonight."

"Always." I'm still holding her hand and I give it a squeeze.

"Shaw, do you remember Steve?" Jonah asks and nods to the other guy.

"You were down last summer?" I ask.

He nods. "Yeah, good memory."

Jonah takes a sip of his beer. "We were just talking about playing quarters. Do you two want in?"

"Uhh..." Shit. I just got Sydney off the ledge from the last competitive game.

"Yes," she answers for us as she elbows me. "Don't give me that look. I'll be fine." Then she mumbles, "As long as no one hits on you."

Chuckling, I let her lead me inside to the dining table. Jonah goes to get supplies while the rest of us take a seat. Sydney's to my left and I scoot my chair closer to her and rest a hand on her leg under the table.

Jonah comes back with Willow at his side. She seems nice and I don't think she's actually trying to piss off my girl, but Sydney stiffens as Willow takes the seat across from me.

"Are you as good at quarters as you are everything else?" she asks, setting her drink on the table in front of her.

"I'm not sure. It's been awhile since I played."

Jonah places a glass in the middle of the table and pops the tab on a beer. He fills it about three quarters of the way. "Who wants to start?"

No one immediately volunteers, but Willow is the first to give. "I'll go."

Jonah slides a quarter down the table. We go all the way around the table once without anyone making it.

"Well, this is going to be the most boring game ever," Jonah says at the same moment Willow takes her second turn and drops the quarter in the glass.

"Fuck, that's coming to me, isn't it?" he asks Willow as she laughs and then passes him the glass.

Willow makes it two more times, forcing me to drink and then Richard.

"You get to make a rule," Steve reminds her.

"Hmmm..." She places a finger on her chin. Her nails are painted yellow and the bright color makes me think of Sydney. Hers are currently white and I wonder if that was also for me. "I'm banning the word drink. If you say the banned word then you have to take a..." Instead of saying the word she motions with her hand like she's taking a drink.

I'm incredibly good at avoiding the word drink in all its variations from playing this game with Datson and our teammates. I learned the way everyone does—the super painful, incredibly drunk way where you pass out downstairs in the middle of the party.

And Sydney's been present for a lot of those games, too, so we get to sit back and laugh as everyone continually trips up and is forced to drink. Richard is especially bad, but the tipsier he gets the more handsy he gets, and Jonah doesn't seem like he minds.

Sydney leans over, her blonde hair acting like a curtain to hide her face from everyone else. "Where's the bathroom?"

"I'll show you." I push my chair back and stand. "We'll be right back."

There's a bathroom on the main floor, but there's a line of girls waiting for it, so I take her upstairs.

"Second door on the left." I hang back at the top of the stairs and let her go ahead.

"Thanks."

I pull out my phone and take a seat on the top stair. Tara called again tonight and left a message for me to call her back so we can make plans for the Fourth. We always do it up big with a party at the house. The last three years have been awesome, and I want this year to be even better.

I shoot Tara a quick text to promise I'll call her soon. I don't hear the bathroom door open or Sydney approaching before her fingers slide over my eyes. I could tell it was her even if she weren't the only other person up here. I'm highly attuned to her touch.

"Eww. Your hands are wet."

"At least you know I washed them." She takes a seat next to me on the stairs. "This house is amazing. What do Jonah's parents do?"

"His dad is a judge. I can't remember if he's ever said what his mom does."

"How did you two meet?"

"We played against each other in high school and AAU. The first weekend I came down here three years ago I ran into him. I couldn't place him, but knew I recognized him from somewhere. Luckily, he remembered me." I shrug. "That was pretty much it. I don't hear from him during the year, but as soon as I get to the lake each summer, we fall back into hanging out. He's a good guy."

"Like us," she says. "We don't usually hang out during school breaks, but when we're at Valley, we always fall back together."

"Not exactly like that." I slide my hand up her leg to her hip and bring my lips to hers. She opens for me immediately and I waste no time sweeping my tongue in her mouth and tasting her. Sydney kisses like it's a competitive sport and she is a gold medal winner every single time.

We're interrupted by someone coming up the stairs and reluctantly, I stand and we head back down. I really don't feel like playing quarters or generally being around anyone but Sydney.

"I have an idea. You game?" I squeeze her hand.

Without even asking for more details she agrees, and with a little creativity and fast thinking, I'm able to mostly create the first date I had planned. I grab all the supplies and lead her into the garage. We sit on the workout bench facing one another.

"What is this?"

"Alternate date number one, of course."

"Date number one was dinner, I take it?" she asks, taking a cheese puff from the bag between us.

"*Is* dinner. I said alternate, but I meant bonus date. The real one will be much classier. No plastic cups or food that comes from a bag. I did picture it a lot like this though. You in a dress, me looking sharp as always."

"The smell of sweat in the air," she says dreamily, holding a hand over her heart and then laughing.

"But it achieves the most important part of my first date—having you all to myself."

"I know somewhere else you could achieve that."

I ignore that obvious reference to sex for the sake of my dick who is looking for any reason to pop up and make it about him.

"What's the best date you've ever been on?" I ask.

"Drinks at a little cafe in Italy."

"Figures fucking Sebastian couldn't even take you on a real date. Drinks is a bullshit excuse for a date."

She rolls her eyes and pops another cheese puff in her mouth. "What's the best date you've ever planned?"

"I haven't."

"I don't understand. They couldn't have all sucked."

"I've never really been on a date like that. Not a real one where I asked a girl out and planned something specifically for her. You know how it is. You make plans with someone and you just sort of show up together at the same place. I'm not counting those."

"What about Amelia? I thought you guys went to a couple concerts and what about the time you took her to the Diamondbacks game?"

"All her. She planned those or told me she wanted to do them and sent me links with dates and times."

"She did the work." As she takes a drink, she nods thought-fully. Then, still holding the drink up to her mouth, says, "I think I finally figured out what all your ex's have in common."

"I'm almost afraid to ask."

"They made it easy on you. They built a relationship and you were along for the ride." That stings a little, but she places the cup on the bench and leans in. "I don't blame you. Your schedule is nuts, and to fit into your life, any girl is going to have to be cool with that, but they each took control so that they never had to wait on you to make a move."

"I've got moves."

"Hello, 'Mister I've never planned a date before'."

"There might be a shred of truth to your theory, but that's all the more reason I want to do it differently with you. I failed to act the first time around, but not now. I've got all sorts of plans."

"All right. I give. Five dates. Real dates that you plan."

"I'm sorry, did you just forfeit something? Where's my best friend and what have you done with her?" I knock my knee against hers playfully.

"I don't need them to know I want something more with you. That hasn't changed. But I want to be good for you in a way those other girls weren't. So, if you need this then you can have it. Clear your schedule after date five though."

Vulnerable, honest, stripped down beyond the bubbly, competitive, fun girl is this other version of Sydney few get to see. She's terrified of letting people down, afraid of failure and being hurt, but she's also one of the bravest people I know and loyal as hell. When she sets her mind to something, there's no stopping her. And she would fight to the death for anyone she cares about.

"You already are good for me."

The next morning, Datson wakes up at an ungodly hour wanting to take the boat out one last time before he heads back to the farm.

I don't wake Sydney. We were up most of the night talking. Well, mostly talking.

The lake is still quiet and my buddy is too. I wish I knew what to say to make him feel better about talking with his family. I can't do it for him any more than he can help me decide, so I do what I can which is drive his ass all around the lake.

We have lunch and then head back so he can get on the road. Sydney is sitting on the patio with a pair of bright green sunglasses that match the smallest bikini I've ever seen. And I've seen some small ones.

My steps falter and I'm almost certain I trip over my tongue like a cartoon character.

"Ah, Syd, you missed a great morning out on the water," Datson says, apparently impervious to the itsy bitsy teeny weenie, hot-green bikini attached to the hottest woman alive.

"Great and morning don't belong in the same sentence," she quips back.

He takes a seat on a chair next to her. I'm still trying to work my feet. She short-circuited whatever part of my brain is responsible for that.

"Look at you two," Datson says, and I think he must have figured out that something's different between us. Possibly because I'm staring like a goddamn idiot. "You've got fucking matching suits. Aren't you two the cutest BFFs ever."

I glance down at my bright green shorts and then back to Sydney. Sure enough.

"These are new. How'd you know?" I ask her.

"I didn't. I bought this yesterday."

"Adorbs." Datson sits forward and claps his hands. "Well, as much as I'd love to third wheel it for another few days, maybe get a glimpse of the hot kisses I keep hearing about but not witnessing, I should get going."

"Thanks for coming. It was good to see you. If you can get away again, you know where to find us. I think Benny and a couple of the younger guys are coming up for the Fourth."

"I appreciate it." He stands and Sydney does too to hug him. "Take care of him."

"Always," she reassures him. When she steps back, she lets her hands fall to his arms at the elbow and squeezes. "Careful driving back."

By the time I walk Datson out to his truck and come back, Sydney's poured us each a drink and reheated leftovers.

"I was hungry. Thought you might be, too."

"Datson and I got lunch." Dropping on the chair, I eat half of the food anyway before speaking again. "What do you want to do tonight?"

"I assumed you had some elaborate plan. If not, I'm good with just hanging at the house."

"Oh, I have a plan. I just wanted to make it seem like you had a choice. We can chill here for a bit, but we leave for official date one at seven."

"Sydney, you look amazing."

I can see the faint blush of her cheeks even in the dim lighting of the restaurant. "Thank you. This place is incredible. Much better than Jonah's garage, though, I had fun last night. Best date material. It's going to be hard to beat it."

"Oh, ye of little faith."

"So, what does the official date one entail?"

"You're looking at it."

She waits for more. She knows me well.

"There's a club upstairs. I doubt there's much action on a Sunday night, but it's supposed to have the best view of the entire lake."

"And?"

My smile is big and immediate. "Boat ride home under the stars."

"You are pretty good at this planning dates thing for a guy who hasn't done it before."

We eat, conversation flows easily, as it always does with us. It doesn't feel like much of a date at all, mostly, but the unfamiliar excitement in my gut and tingling through my fingertips as I press a hand to her lower back and lead her upstairs is the stuff of first dates that I didn't realize I was missing out on. Though to be fair, I'm not sure I'd feel this way with anyone but Sydney.

It isn't like there weren't good times with Amelia, but Sydney's right. I let her, and everyone else I dated, run the show. I treated dates almost like they were a reward for putting up with my insane schedule and the hundreds of nights they came over and just chilled because I couldn't go out because of a practice or game the next day.

That's my life. In between a fun night out once a week or once every few weeks when things are really busy, is a lot of nights of me going to bed early so I can be at my best. Letting my girlfriends pick the dates felt like the least I could do. Now I have to wonder if I should have been more excited to plan things like I am now.

Seeing Sydney's face when we get to the balcony on the top floor of this club tells me everything I need to know. One, planning dates for her is fun. Two, I don't want to go back to relationships where I'm a passive participant. And three, fuck all my good intentions and reasons for holding out.

Chapter Sixteen
SYDNEY

Tanner grabs me a drink from the bar and we sit on a low sofa on the balcony. It's a clear night and the moon and stars create a light show on the lake. I lean into him to steal some of his warmth and he pulls me closer.

"It's amazing up here." The wind blows my hair around my face and into Tanner's.

"I'm not sure how you can even see it." He uses both hands to brush my hair out of my face.

Goose bumps dot my arms as he continues to touch me and look at me like I'm the only other person out here. Something changed over dinner. One minute we were Tanner and Sydney, best friends who want more, and the next we were two people on a first date with insane chemistry ready to rip each other's clothes off. I can see it on his face. No matter how hard he's trying to hide it or stick to his five-date plan. He's breaking.

"Cold?" He rubs my arms from shoulder to wrist.

"I'm okay."

"Liar. Your nipples are saluting me." His gaze falls to my chest, as does mine.

I press against him and he wraps me up so that his chin rests on top of my head. "I really dig your boobs. Especially when they're rubbing against me."

A burst of laughter escapes and I lift my head forcing him to create enough space so I can look him in the eye. "Really? They're so small." I push them out and his blue eyes watch with rapt interest.

"They're perfect... and now I'm hard." With a groan, he stands and takes my hand. "Dance with me."

That seems like the worst way to get rid of a boner, but what do I know? The dance floor is practically empty. It isn't that late – definitely not clubbing hour, and it is Sunday night. Most people are probably home resting up for the week or recovering from the weekend.

The few other people out here care about us as much as we do them, though. We're all in our own little bubbles. Tanner's a good dancer. He doesn't do it much back at Valley, but on a few drunken occasions, I've been able to pull him onto a frat party dance floor.

Moving to the beat, he keeps one hand on my hip, holding on to the spandex fabric of my dress like he's keeping me from moving farther away. As if I'd try.

I lean into the touch wanting more. So much more. He gives it to me, spreading his long fingers out so they splay out over my rib cage. The heat of him and his familiar scent vibrate through me with the music.

We're in sync without trying. Each time I move closer, so does he, until we're chest to chest. I rest my arms on his shoulders, and he now has both hands on either side of my waist.

We're junior high dancing. The kind where our hands are in appropriate places, but the bad intentions fill the space between us. Hormones and indecisions are so thick it's hard to breathe.

Tilting my head up, I bring our lips close. His gaze darts to my mouth and his eyes darken. This is it. He's going to kiss me again. It has to be him. I've made the move too many times.

"Come on, there's some place else I want to dance with you." He takes off, pulling me behind him without waiting for a response.

I fight off the sting of disappointment that he's able to hold back when I feel like I'll die from unrequited lust. I need him in a way that is about so much more than sex.

The club is set up so that the dance floor and bar are inside, and the seating area, where we were sitting earlier, is outside on the balcony so it's quieter and easier to talk. I think that's where he's leading me, but instead he stalks out of the club, down through the restaurant, and back outside the way we came in a couple of hours ago.

I'm curious, but keep my questions to myself as he holds on tight to my hand while speed walking to the boat. Helping me on board, he says, "I'll apologize later for the abrupt ending to our first date, but I needed to do this without an audience."

His mouth slams onto mine catching me by surprise, but breaking the small amount of control I was holding up. I press back, attacking his mouth in a desperate way, trying to convey just how much I want this. I'll let him lead because I know it's important to him, but he'll have no doubt how much I want him.

His grip on my body is possessive and demanding. Those big hands roam over my waist and back, and thread through my hair. The thing about Tanner's insistence to do everything the right way this time (besides being incredibly sexually frustrating) is that in trying to give me exactly what I want, he's doing the opposite. I *want* to get naked, dammit.

People change. Their needs and wants evolve with time and experiences. Two years ago, I was a girl who was terrified of getting her heart broken again, but I'm not that girl anymore. I've realized in that time that I've broken my own heart more times than anyone else. I've let people walk all over me, I've been afraid to ask for what I want, and I've dated people who were all wrong for me because I couldn't risk wanting my best friend and having him reject me a second time.

"Fuck, kissing you isn't enough." He rests his forehead against mine. Our chests lift with each ragged breath. "I was afraid I was two seconds away from mouth fucking you on the middle of the dance floor."

"That would have livened up that place, for sure."

"Yeah, sorry it was a little quiet tonight. We'll come back another time when it's busier."

"Not necessary. I would have blocked them all out anyway. You have that effect on me, you know? I forget other people are around."

"Same." He grins.

I sit across from him with my feet up on the side of his seat as he drives back to the house. He keeps one hand resting on my ankle. The fifteen-minute ride felt short on the way here, but the anticipation building as Tanner guides us home in the dark makes every minute feel longer than the last.

I'm starting to get the hang of this whole boat thing, so I help him tie up at the dock. As soon as we're done, Tanner lifts me into his arms by sweeping my feet out from under me and carrying me against his chest back onto the boat. "I promised you dancing and stars," he says, stopping and looking up.

It really is a beautiful night. He sets me down and I wrap my arms around his neck. There's no music and I'm definitely not looking at the stars, but as our bodies come together and sway in the dark, it's perfect. A moment in time that I know I'll never forget.

"It was a good date." I rest my head on his shoulder. His cologne has all but worn off, just the faintest hint of it lingers.

Despite all my efforts to throw myself at him to somehow make up for holding back years ago and show him how ready I am, he's managed to give me something I didn't even know I wanted. He's made me feel special. Extremely frustrated? Yes. But also extremely special.

"Thank you for this. Seriously, tonight has been so much more than I expected."

"What, like you expected it to suck?" he asks with a laugh.

"No, I knew that we would have fun, we always do, but I feel closer to you in a different way. It feels real. I'm probably not explaining it very well."

"Nah, I get it. I wish I could say that was all part of my master plan, but I just wanted to give you a real first date. I feel it too, though."

"So, two dates down. What's next?"

"*One* date down. Nice try."

"How about a friendly wager?"

He smirks. "No, way, babe. You're dating me. Get used to disappointment." He stops. "Wait, that came out wrong."

"Hear me out. If I can guess date number two then we make the official date count two. Last night was amazing, cheese puffs and all. It should count as a date."

He smiles, showing his perfectly straight teeth and full lips. He rarely smiles with teeth and I love it when he does. "You'll never guess date number two. Date one was traditional first date material, but date two..." He shakes his head and makes a face like the idea of me guessing what goes on in his brain is absolutely ludicrous.

"Then you have nothing to worry about."

"All right, fine. You know what? I'm planning on taking you on a lot more than five dates in the future so any which way you count it, we've only scratched the surface. Guess away."

"Really?" I shouldn't be this excited, but the idea of winning something combined with getting naked one day sooner has me all sorts of giddy.

"Three guesses. No hints."

We're still standing in the middle of the boat swaying gently under the moonlight. It's quiet except for the occasional boat going by.

I'm almost positive I know what the next date is. He thinks he's hard to read, but he isn't. Not to me.

Date one was traditional and romantic. Dinner, dancing, the boat ride. Whatever he has planned next will be lighter and more us. Our best times together are silly, fun, and playful, and I guarantee that worked its way into his dates, even if only subconsciously.

"Mini golf?"

"Nope," he says a little too proudly.

"Jet skis or something water related."

He shakes his head, a super smug smile pulling his lips so high I can now see his gums in addition to those pearly whites. "Wrong again."

Crap. I was so certain it was one of those. I really don't think I'm wrong about it being something athletic and fun, though. I'm at a slight disadvantage not knowing everything the lake has to offer, but I think back to everything he's told me and the little bit I saw when I went out on my own.

Or maybe all five dates are like date one. Maybe he assumed we'd do playful and fun all on our own and kept the theme of the dates super romantic. I really want to guess right for reasons that really have nothing to do with the date count. Stupid competitive nature. Okay, think, Sydney.

"A tiny hint?" I plead.

"Oh no, no way."

I growl deep in my throat which just makes him laugh.

"Oooh, I've got it. Bowling!" I saw an adorable bowling place in the strip mall. Bright neon lights. It looked super fun and Tanner and I actually went bowling once with the guys. It was a great night that ended with me sleeping over and us talking half the night. We learned so much about each other and it was when I finally felt like we'd worked past whatever could have been and become real friends.

I'm so sure of my choice and excited too, but Tanner shakes his head. "Damn, that would have been a good idea. Remember that time we went years ago with Nathan and Chloe? I think even Joel and Katrina came. That was a good night, but that's not what we're doing for date three." His big smile falls. "Shit, having you guess just makes me realize how many dates I want to take you on. We're gonna do it all, babe. Just you wait."

Chapter Seventeen

SYDNEY

I'm doing some yoga and light stretches on the deck. It's so peaceful out here during the day. I'm starting to think I could get used to this whole lake life thing. The weekends are crazy. The roughly twenty to thirty-five age demographic drives down with their friends, and the lake, as well as the bars, are packed. During the week there are still people out, but it's a lot more families than singles and the feel is different, less chaotic and more chill.

When I finish up, I roll the mat and head inside.

"Tanner?" I call to the empty living area. He went to grab some more groceries, but I see the empty paper bags on the counter, but no Tanner.

"Bedroom."

I follow his voice and walk in on him pulling his T-shirt over his head. The movement ruffles his hair. He balls up the white material and tosses it in the hamper.

"How's the shoulder?" he asks.

"It's feeling better. I'm going to see the physical therapist again tomorrow. I miss volleyball."

He walks toward me. The muscles in his chest and stomach flex with each step. "You'll be back and better than ever soon. I'm going to hop in the shower and then if you're game, take you on date number two."

"A day date?" I smile wide, already excited for whatever he has planned. "I'm game. Do I get a hint yet?"

"Nope." He takes out his phone and tosses it on the bed.

"At least tell me what I should wear."

"That feels like cheating."

Rolling my eyes, I sigh. "Dress? Shorts? Bikini? Heels? Flip-flops? Tennis shoes?"

There's a faraway look on his face as I talk. "Tanner?" I wave a hand in front of his face.

"Sorry." He snaps out of it. "I was picturing you in all those things. I really want to say bikini and heels..." He looks up toward the ceiling and smiles. "The bright orange one and your hot pink heels... yeah." He nods.

I try to bite back a laugh and fail. "Your brain is a scary place."

"Shhh. You're ruining it." He presses a finger to my lips and keeps his gaze on the ceiling.

I swat his hand away and he finally breaks out of the trance. "Shorts and tennis shoes." He sighs dramatically. "But keep the orange bikini and pink heels ready for date four."

Well, that sparks my curiosity, but he heads off toward the bathroom. The shower starts as Tanner's phone begins ringing.

"Your phone's going off," I yell to him.

"Can you answer it for me? It's my sister. She's been calling every day to make plans for the Fourth."

I grab it off the bed and take it to the open bathroom door. "Here."

He pokes his head out of the shower curtain. "My hands are wet. Answer it and tell her I'll call her back."

I hesitate and he adds, "Otherwise she'll just keep on calling. She's annoying like that."

He disappears back into the shower. Silently clearing my throat, I put the phone to my ear and answer. "Hey, Tara. It's, uh, Sydney. Tanner's in the shower."

"Sydney. Hi." There's an awkward pause. "I didn't realize you were still there." She sounds less friendly than I imagined, but I figure that's to be expected since she called her brother and someone else answered.

"Oh, yeah, hey," I say cheerily. I've never met Tara or even spoken to her and this is not how I pictured it. "I hear you're coming to the lake next week. I'm so excited to finally meet you."

"Yeah, uh, you too. Can you have Tanner call me when he gets out of the shower?"

"Definitely. He wanted me to tell you that." My face warms and I feel awful for reasons I can't quite pinpoint. Maybe I expected her to be more excited? But I have no idea how much Tanner has told her about me.

"Thanks."

"You're welcome. Good to finally meet you or talk to you," I babble on feeling determined to get some pleasantries out of this girl that seems awfully put out by having to talk to me. "You know what I mean."

She doesn't budge, though. "I do. Bye now." Her tone isn't hostile, but incredibly bland and detached.

"Bye." I step back into the bathroom and set his phone on the vanity. "She wants you to call."

"Cool. Thanks."

"I'm going to get ready," I say to the closed curtain and duck back out.

I replay the call as I get dressed for our date. Perhaps it was unrealistic to think Tanner told his sister anything about me. They're just so close that I guess I assumed that my name came up occasionally if only in passing.

I'm still trying to shake the uneasy feeling as Tanner drives to our second date. He looks as gorgeous as ever in navy shorts and a gray V-neck. He hangs a right off the main road in town. "Ready?"

He comes to a stop in front of a large outdoor sports complex.

"Which one are we doing?" From the car I can see go karts, bumper boats, and paintball.

We get out of the car and meet in front. "All of them, if you want, but we're starting at the batting cages."

"Glad I didn't wear my bikini and heels."

"It's a real great visual, not going to lie, but I thought you might not appreciate being ogled while trying to hit my fast ball."

"You're going to pitch to me?"

He nods, a charming boyish grin on his face. "Mhmm. Don't worry, I'll let you warm up with the machine first. I throw much harder."

Once we've paid, I stand behind the cage while he warms up with the machine. He takes cut after cut, hitting the ball into the net on the opposite end. I could watch him like this all day. Totally in his element and showing off for me.

"Hey, batter, batter," I say through the chain-link fence.

"Are you ready to give it a try?" he asks, briefly looking over his shoulder before hitting the next ball. The machine stops and he backs out of the cage. He takes the helmet in my hand

and forces it onto my head, then kisses me. "Yep, a bikini would have really made this fantasy complete."

"Your mind really is a scary place, isn't it?"

He winks and motions with his head to the cage. "Get in there."

I grab a bat inside and hit the button to start the machine. I haven't swung a bat since... high school gym class maybe? I'm giving myself a pep talk when the first pitch comes flying by me. I swing, but it's almost too late and I only get a small piece of the ball sending it off to the right.

Tanner doesn't comment or offer any advice. I don't look back, but out of my peripheral, I can see his arms overhead, fingers hooked into the fence as he watches on. I narrow my focus and concentrate hard. I'm able to make contact with each pitch, but they look nothing like his perfect hits straight down the line.

Is it ridiculous to be frustrated that I can't hit a baseball as well as a division one college baseball player? Yes. Am I anyway? Also yes.

I don't realize how tightly I'm gripping the bat or how sweaty I am until strong arms wrap around me from behind. "Easy, killer. This is supposed to be fun."

I loosen my hold as I watch one go by. "Yeah, yeah, I just want to hit one really good."

"You're swinging too late." He steps back. "Get ready. I'll tell you when."

Letting out a deep breath, another ball flies by while I prepare.

"This one's yours, babe. You got this."

I nod. His words light up something inside of me that my own pep talk didn't. The ball appears along with the sound the machine makes as it releases each pitch.

"Now," Tanner says.

It feels too early. I want to hold back, but my body is more cooperative than my brain. I swing, connecting with the ball and sending it sailing straight down the middle. A zap of pride and joy shoots through me just like when I make a perfect serve in volleyball. There's no other feeling like it.

I turn to him while practically bouncing with excitement. "I hit it!"

"I saw."

"Like really hit it."

His blue eyes are twinkling with laughter, but he holds it in. I go to hug him and forget about all the accessories. My helmet bangs against his and I nearly get him in the groin with the end of the bat.

"Oops, sorry." I step back but I'm still giddy. "That is amazing. I want to do it again."

We move from the machine to an area where Tanner can pitch to me. He stands behind a safety screen per the rules, but it's almost laughable because I don't stand a chance of hitting anything he sends my way. And actually I don't mind. Not much.

He looks too good to complain. He's carefree and happy.

"All right. This one is for you."

"What were the last twenty?"

He holds the ball up. "Me showing off for my date."

He throws a couple much slower pitches until I get a few good hits. Back outside of the cages, we return our bats and helmets.

"Now what?" I ask.

"Your pick."

We wander past the cages. The different games are set up in a semicircle that arcs around the parking lot.

"I feel like I should get credit since they do have mini golf here," I point out as we pass the course with bright colored obstacles and fun water hazards.

"I avoided anything where we had to play against one another for a reason. Tell me, when you've gone on dates with guys what did they say when they saw sweet, beautiful Sydney turn into the gold-medal monster?"

"I may have played it down. It wasn't easy."

Chuckling, he squeezes my hand. "You don't have to hide anything from me."

My heart rate speeds up and my stomach flips. "What about you? Do you let girls win on dates?"

He doesn't answer right away and looks a little guilty.

"You totally have!" I smack his arm playfully. "I did not think you were the type. You've never let me win anything."

"You're different. I've never dated anyone like you."

"I don't know how to respond to that. I can't tell if that's a compliment or if I should be worried."

"Definitely a compliment."

We make a complete circle before deciding on bumper boats and get in the line to wait our turn.

"Did you talk to your sister?" I lean back against the metal railing.

"Yeah, I called her while you were getting ready." Nothing about his body language suggests she said anything about our awkward encounter.

"Everything good?"

"She just wanted to talk about the Fourth. She and her friend Corinne are coming down and it sounds like a few of her teammates might too. We're going to have quite a houseful."

"I never really asked, but is it cool that I'm here crashing your summer plans?"

"I invited you, remember?" One brow quirks up.

"I know, but doesn't your family take issue with some free-loader they've never met staying at their fabulous lake house all summer?"

"No." He steps forward as the line moves. "Tara never comes without Corinne or one of her other friends. The lake is much more fun when you can enjoy it with other people."

"I'm nervous about meeting her," I admit.

"Don't be. Aside from being a giant pain in my ass, she's cool. You two will get along."

He's right. I don't know why I'm letting one weird phone call freak me out. I'm excited to finally meet his sister, and if she's even half as amazing as Tanner, I know I'll like her just fine.

Chapter Eighteen

TANNER

"Got you two a present." Jonah tosses a heart-shaped raft into the pool. It has two hearts and they're connected in the middle. He's got a smug look on his face and his eyes crinkle up at the corners with humor.

"Jokes on you. This thing is baller," I say as I heft myself up onto the bigger heart.

Sydney looks reluctant but with a shake of her head, she gets on the other side.

It took all of five seconds for Jonah to figure out things had changed between us. I'm actually surprised he didn't notice the other night at his party, but I guess that's because he was focused on Richard.

"That's fucking precious." Jonah stands on the side of the pool and holds up his phone like he's going to take a picture.

I lean over and take Sydney by surprise when I press my mouth to hers. We spent all morning lying in bed kissing. My lips are chapped and I'm more frustrated than I've been in my entire life, but I wouldn't change a thing.

"So," Ollie says as he swims over to us with a giant, mocking smile. "What's date number three?"

I look from him to Jonah to Sydney. "What? How? You told them?"

She shrugs and tries to look sweet and innocent.

"Don't hold out on us," Ollie begs.

"Holding out is sort of your new thing, huh?" Jonah jumps in. He runs a hand through his wet hair, slicking back the dark red strands.

"You told them *that*?!"

Sydney grimaces and looks over at me with apologetic brown eyes. "I thought you'd already told them."

Playing both sides to get more information. I should have known. Classic Jonah.

"Tell us! What's date number three? I've got my money on karaoke." Ollie looks so certain and I have no clue where he'd get such an idea.

Jonah laughs. "No way. I've heard Shaw sing. I'm going with the movies. Sharing a bowl of popcorn, their fingers touch in the dark..."

"No," Sydney pipes in. Three heads swivel to her. "You're both wrong. It's something more romantic like a candlelight dinner on the boat or a picnic, also with candles."

"So, your guess is he planned candles?" Jonah asks with a smirk. "Shaw? Which one is it?"

"I do like candles." I kick my foot along the water sending a spray of water at Jonah. "I'm not telling."

"Come on!" The three of them take turns whining and trying to get me to tell them.

"We should do a double date. Nay, a triple date." Ollie elbows Jonah. "You could invite Richard and maybe Jade?"

"Oh no, if you didn't close that last weekend, then you're

on your own, but I would love to see this date. Come on, Shaw, let us crash."

"A group date could be fun." Sydney smiles. That smile makes me want to give her anything she asks for. "Does that work for what you had planned? If not, we could do another bonus date."

I don't answer right away, torn between admitting the truth and making up something on the spot.

"Well?" Ollie asks. "What's date three?"

"Movie theater," I grumble.

Jonah and Sydney crack up and I hide behind my shades.

"Good call. Someplace you can't talk too much and screw it up." Ollie nods in understanding. "Plus, popcorn."

We go to the late show and I must admit that going with a group was more fun than I expected.

"Where's Richard tonight?" I ask Jonah. Sydney and Ollie are walking ahead of us as we head to the ice cream place next door to the theater.

"He and the band are in California for some festival."

"Is he coming back?"

"Maybe." Jonah shrugs his big shoulders, hands in his pocket.

"Sorry, man."

"It's cool."

I'm not convinced, but I leave it alone.

"Why five dates?"

I was waiting for him to give me shit for this. Surprised it took this long.

"When we first met, she'd been burned by this guy and had

a rule that she wouldn't sleep with a guy until they'd been on five dates."

"And you weren't willing to wait? That doesn't seem like you."

"No. I was, I did, but I wasn't clear about it. We hung out real casual and I assumed that was enough. I was so used to girls just throwing themselves at me that I guess I didn't take it all that seriously. The more time that went by, the more I liked her. I was waiting for some sort of sign that she was ready, that I'd put in enough time for her to trust me, all the while she was waiting for me to make a move. Eventually she started dating other people, and I realized I fucked-up, but it was too late, the moment had passed."

"Brutal."

"Yeah." I look ahead where Sydney's smiling at Ollie, the two of them are carrying on like old friends.

"Five real dates to make up for the ones you didn't take her on two years ago. That's pretty romantic, Shaw."

"Well, she deserves it. Better late than never."

"For what it's worth, she knows how much you care about her. I think she even knows how much you regret two years ago."

"I know she doesn't need five dates to prove that I want her. She's told me *many* times, but I want it to be perfect for her. I want to make up for everything I should have done. Two years..." I rarely let myself go down the *what could have been* road because it ends with this pit in my stomach full of disgust and remorse. "I could have kept her from dating a whole slew of douchebags, shielded her from the pain each time things didn't work. I could have made her happy."

"Regret is a funny thing. It often makes us do things for all the wrong reasons, chase ideals that don't matter, and all for ourselves. Regret is selfish."

"What are you saying?"

"She just wants you, man. She doesn't care about the regrets you have. She has her own and the only thing they have in common is that you want to be together now. Nothing either of you do now is going to change the past." He claps me on the shoulder before we catch up to Sydney and Ollie.

"Are you ready?" Jonah asks Ollie. He motions with his head to the parking lot. "I thought we could go by The Cove and catch last call."

"Now? We're just about to order."

Jonah laughs. "I think we've crashed enough of this date. Come on, I'll buy you a beer."

With a sigh, Ollie steps out of line. "Baller date three, Shaw. I would have definitely put out."

"Thanks, man. It was fun." I wrap both arms around Sydney's waist from behind. "See you guys later."

At the counter, she orders a vanilla cone and I get mint chocolate chip in a bowl. Circular tables are set up on the far side of the building, and I lead Sydney to one of the unoccupied ones. We sit side by side eating in silence. Her hair is pulled back in a ponytail, but the wind blows the blonde strands into my face.

"Sorry," she says as she takes the end and twirls it around in her fist and holding it to the other side as she continues to lick the sweet dessert in her other hand.

The number of times I've thought about fisting her hair just like that are far too many to count. I'd like to kick myself for not doing it years ago. How different might the last two years have been if I had?

"What?" Sydney asks.

I realize I'm staring at her while lost in my thoughts. I don't want to bring the night down with talk of the past, though.

"What are your plans for after graduation?"

"I don't know. I'd like to do something with volleyball, maybe coach a youth team or even just volunteer. The volleyball coach at my old high school is retiring after this year. They've all but offered me the job, but I can't see myself there."

I can't picture her there either. I can't picture her anywhere but with me, wherever I am.

"Where do you see yourself?" I ask.

"I'm not sure. I like the city but being close to the beach would be nice. Maybe traveling. I like the idea of jumping around a bit, seeing the world."

"I can picture you doing that."

She lifts one shoulder in a small shrug. "Well, it isn't exactly a plan, but I'll have a degree in graphic design and I can do that almost anywhere. There are a lot of contract and remote jobs so I could live wherever I want. What about you? Have you decided yet?"

"No. I promised myself I wouldn't spend the summer obsessing about it and that's been pretty easy with you here. Am I crazy if I want to continue to do both sports?" She's the only person I've really asked their opinion. Everyone else has asked mine, given me advice, but not Sydney, she's made it clear that she'll support me no matter what, but she's never told me what she thinks I should do.

"Is that what you want?"

"Yeah, of course. That's always been my dream, but actually pulling it off?" I push my ice cream around with the spoon.

"If anyone can do it, it's you. You're incredible."

I don't voice my other concern that has absolutely nothing to do with getting drafted by two pro sports. How am I going to do that and have Sydney by my side? Or any girl for that matter.

It isn't a life people dream about. The money, the fame, sure, but not the reality of it. Gone more often than not, ready to pick up your life and move any time you're traded... it's a lonely life for a significant other. Or so Tara tells me. She's super into those reality TV shows about NBA players' wives. Keeping someone else happy was never my concern. Selfish or not, I've worked hard to make my dreams a reality. But now... I wonder if Sydney could see herself living like that?

But it's the last summer of fun and I'm no more anxious to answer that question than I am to decide my own future.

Back at the house, Sydney heads for her room instead of mine. "I'm going to shower and change."

"All right. I'll leave the door open if you want to come back and cuddle."

Stepping back to me, she presses her mouth to mine kissing me and then pulling back but letting her lips linger close. "Thank you for tonight. I had a great time."

"Me too, babe. Always."

She closes the door behind her as she goes. In my room, I flop onto the bed and lay on my back. I kick off my shoes and continue to stare up at the ceiling in the dark.

Restless. Anxious. Frustrated.

I can handle the emotions, but now I wonder if Jonah's onto something. Feeding my regret of the past by holding back in the present, what good does that do? I fucked-up years ago and there's nothing I can do to change that, but I can show her now.

Fuck. I move to a stand so quick I get a little lightheaded.

My legs eat up the space between our rooms. I knock hoping she'll hear me over the shower. "Syd?"

"One minute."

I can hear her rustling around in the bedroom so she's definitely not in the shower yet. I don't really have a plan. Fuck her senseless. It's a good start anyway.

When she opens the door, it's only a crack and I can tell immediately something's going on. The uneasiness is written all over her pretty face. "What's up?"

"Is everything okay?" I try to see past her.

"Yeah, um..." She rolls her bottom lip behind her teeth.

"Babe?"

Her grip on the door lessens and I push it open. The room is lit with candles—ones I'm pretty sure go in the bathroom. My mom has them sprinkled all over this place. Her feet are bare, but she's still in the dress she wore out. She holds a deck of cards in her hands. "I wanted to surprise you. Listen, I know you have a plan for our first five dates—"

"Change of plans."

Chapter Nineteen

SYDNEY

My mouth opens on a yelp that Tanner catches with his tongue. With no warmup or pretense, this kiss is hard and demanding and makes his intentions clear. Or maybe I'm just being hopeful.

His hands slide down my back and dip below my butt, and he hoists me up into his arms. I wrap my legs around him, and he walks us back to the bed. He lays me down gently, never breaking the kiss.

I don't know what changed tonight, but I'm beyond ready. I want him. I've wanted him for two years—no even before that—but now I want him in all the same ways plus a million ways I never imagined before this time together at the lake.

With greedy fingers, I fumble for the hem of his T-shirt and lift. He stops only long enough to let me pull it over his head. I toss it and his mouth slams back down on mine. His skin is warm to the touch and I glide my palms over his hard muscles. Tanner has the kind of body that demands attention and respect. I give it both.

Excitement and nerves, the sheer gravity of what's happening makes my breaths come too fast.

"Air," I choke out. "Oh my god, I just got really nervous. We're going to do this, aren't we?"

He stops, those dark blue eyes stare down at me. "Do you not want to?"

I scramble to sit up, and he sits back on his feet.

"No, I do. I *so* do. It's just... what if it's bad? Or it's so good we never leave this bed again? Or the rumor is true and you're so big that it's not physically possible for us to consummate?"

He shakes with laughter. "Consummate?"

"It's a word!"

Tanner tries and fails to stop laughing. He clears his throat a few times and finally gets himself under control.

"Babe, it's us. Of course it's going to be amazing, but we don't have anywhere to be for two weeks. I promise by then no matter how good it is, you'll be ready to leave the bed. And if not, we'll drop out of school and live here in our dirty sex sheets."

"And the other thing?"

His lips twitch. "It'll fit."

My gaze drops to his jeans, and I reach out and unbutton them, then slide the zipper down until I can see the band of his black boxer briefs and his very large bulge. Seriously, he's huge or stuffing socks down there. I was only slightly exaggerating when I said I was worried about it fitting. The guys talk about how big he is almost as much as the girls.

He's so still I'm not sure he's breathing as I move my fingers down to cup him through the cotton material. When I reach my target, he groans low in his throat. Warmth and need spread through me with delicious pleasure. Tanner isn't even touching me, but I feel him in every cell of my being.

"Well, I've confirmed the rumors," I say and swallow thickly. Slowly, I slide the material down as far as I can. Tanner helps by moving to stand beside the bed and together we strip him of his boxers and jeans.

He's beautiful. Long and thick. A bead of precum has gathered at the tip and I lean forward and swipe my tongue along the head. His ab muscles contract making his six-pack and the V along his hips more defined.

At his sides, his hands are curled into fists. The force makes the veins in his hands and forearms more prominent. Dark blue eyes are intently focused on my every move. He's letting me have this—holding back so I feel comfortable, allowing me to control the pace. His dick twitches in front of me.

"That's fun. It's like he's waving."

Tanner's head tilts back and he looks up. Some of the tension leaves his body as he chuckles. "I'm pretty sure he's begging."

"Oh yeah? What does he want?"

He goes from laughing to serious in a flash. "Your mouth," he says gruffly.

As I move closer, his left hand slides through my hair at the nape of my neck. He makes a fist, holding my head tight and tender as I take him in my mouth.

"Dreamed of this so many times."

I know that it's true, that he wouldn't make something like that up, but hearing it sounds so crazy. All this time we could have been doing this. I could have given him so many blow jobs by now.

Gliding down his length, I keep my eyes on him. The hard set to his jaw and the bobbing of his Adam's apple. He groans and then mutters, "So good."

I'm starting to get into it. Taking a little more and swirling my tongue along the underside. He continues to praise me with grunts and moans that light up my confidence and encourage me. Tears well in my eyes as I attempt to deep throat him.

The hand in my hair tightens and guides me up as his mouth crashes down on me. We tumble back onto the bed. While he kisses me, his hands roam down my body to the hem of my dress. All this shuffling has bunched the material up to my hips, but he tugs harder, trying to bring it up higher.

"Torture device," he says against my lips.

"What?"

"Your dresses are torture devices. The bright colors and the way they mold to your curves. They make me crazy." His head dips lower and he kisses a trail down my neck and chest then over the material, nipping and pulling like he's taking his punishment out on the material.

When he's gathered the spandex around my belly button and it isn't going any farther, I sit up and help him get it over my head.

I hadn't thought about being self-conscious until I realize he's having a stare off with my boobs. Every second he doesn't blink I worry that he doesn't like what he sees.

"Hello there," he whispers.

"Ummm... hi?"

"Shh. I wasn't talking to you." He brings a hand up and stretches his palm over one breast. Then the other. With a goofy grin on his face he squeezes and tweaks the nipple. Those long fingers finally slide down over my stomach and hips, around to my butt, which he also squeezes.

It's harder than expected to stay still while he so thoroughly scopes me out. My heart is racing, and I have so much adrenaline and desire pulsing through my veins.

"This is gonna be fun," he says as his arm hooks around my lower back and brings me down onto the mattress.

His naked body stretches out and covers mine for the first time. Our kisses become less playful. We cling to one another. I claw at him and wrap my legs around him trying to get even closer.

"A thousand things I want to do to you." He tries to pull back but my hold on him is too tight for him to get very far. "Need to get condoms."

"Under the pillow."

With a sly smile, he checks beneath the pillow and pulls out a sleeve of condoms.

"There's no nightstand in here," I say with a shrug.

He tears one off and tosses the rest on the floor. He's quick to rip the wrapper open with his teeth and then cover himself with the latex, but he pauses once he's ready and stares down at me.

"What's wrong?" I ask when it seems like too much time has gone by without him moving.

"Not a damn thing."

The head of his cock pushes at my entrance and I hold my breath. So does he, I think. Brow knit with concentration and jaw set tightly, Tanner fills me so completely I'm not sure I can move.

"Oh, fuck, babe, you're so tight." He drops his head forward and mutters a string of curses. "Bet me I can't last more than a minute?"

"Bet you?" I giggle and my body grips him tighter. We both groan at the intensified sensation.

"Use that competitiveness for the greater good."

"I bet you can't last more than three minutes."

"I didn't say ask for a miracle." Those blue eyes meet mine with humor and passion. His smile falls slowly as he somehow buries himself farther inside of me.

My body hums and stretches. I arch into him to create more friction and to see what reactions I can elicit from him. There's something insanely empowering about being responsible for the look of drugged pleasure on his face.

Tanner nuzzles between my boobs. "Are you counting? Has it been one minute? Can I move yet?"

"And sixty," I say like I've been keeping track this entire time.

I'm sure he knows I haven't, but my words encourage him all the same. There's no slow build up, no sweet kisses—there'll be time for all of that later. Right now, it's a race for release.

He grabs my hips on either side as he pumps harder. His mouth skims my skin, teeth graze my navel and then my breasts.

The noises coming out of Tanner are completely unintelligible but his grip on my body and the tempo say everything. My orgasm builds and it's hard to keep my eyes from falling closed or rolling back in my head, but I've never seen anything more spectacular than Tanner on the brink of unraveling.

I gasp and moan, so close I can't hold off any longer. "Tanner," I cry out.

"Babe. Oooh Fuck."

Our combined moans and grunts take us both over the edge. I sink back into the mattress and Tanner flops beside me. He blows out a long breath and my chest rises and falls as I try to catch my breath.

"More than three minutes of that might kill me." I fight to fill my lungs back up with air.

He barks out a laugh and rolls over onto his side, throwing an arm over my middle.

Laying there together, we survey the damage. Clothes strewn around the room, and the pretty floral comforter is askew. It's really no wonder we didn't start a fire.

"It was the candles that broke you, right?" I ask of my weak attempt to set the mood in here. The only candles in this house are those large, three wick ones.

A surprised laugh erupts from his chest and he rolls to face me. "It was you. The candles are a nice touch, though. I do love candles. Though I am not digging whatever that scent is."

"Eucalyptus and pear."

"I gotta get rid of this," he says and gets up and disappears into the bathroom to dispose of the condom. He comes back with a washcloth in one hand and another candle in the other. "Three more of these under the cabinet. How do you feel about vanilla birch?"

"It can't be worse."

He lights the candle and sets it on the floor next to the other one. He sits on the edge of the bed and carefully he runs the damp cloth over my inner thighs and over my pussy. All the nerve endings bloom back to the surface. Once he's finished, he follows it up by dropping open-mouth kisses along my hips and lower stomach. His nose edges down along my clit and then his tongue darts out.

I squirm underneath him. His arms loop around my legs and push them farther apart as he settles between my thighs. He's in no rush this time. Every swipe of his tongue, suction, and nibble is done at a leisurely pace.

It's no matter, though. He brings me to the brink quickly

all the same. I grind against his mouth and tug at the thick strands of hair on his head.

This time, when the orgasm rips through me, I can't even remember his name let alone call it out. I fall back boneless and satiated.

"I can't believe we could have been doing this all along. I want to kick myself."

"I thought the same thing earlier," I say, eyes closed. "It doesn't matter. We'll make up for all of it and then some."

Since neither of us has much in the way of energy, we warm up food and bring it to bed. We sit up talking and eating. We don't bother getting dressed. Legs crossed and knees touching, we share what's left of the two-day-old takeout.

"I think I like that one better," I say around a mouthful of food and nod toward his.

"Here, last bite." He extends the fork toward me and I take it.

He sets the empty container on the bed. "What do you say about taking the boat out tomorrow?"

"Sure, that sounds fun. I can work on my tan."

His gaze drops to my boobs again. For as self-conscious as I am about them, he seems to like them just fine, tan lines and all.

"You misunderstood. I want to teach you to take her out. But I won't complain if you want to be a topless captain. Captainess? Is there a feminine version of captain? Captainette?"

"Really?!"

"Yeah. We've got two weeks left, plus our annual trips, thought you might want to know how."

A vision of us ten years from now out on the water

together, me driving and him kicked back looking happy and relaxed dances in my mind.

Captain or passenger, I don't really care as long as we hold on to that promise to see each other. Everything beyond that just doesn't matter.

We don't make it out of bed the next morning. Not the afternoon either. Sometime midmorning I declared that no one could leave the bed all day except to go to the bathroom. A day filled with all the sex.

"Do you want to go out for dinner?" Tanner asks as he traces small circles on my stomach, his head resting on my chest.

"You mean like get dressed and leave the house?"

He gently bites the peak of one breast. "Technically, I still owe you two dates, and we can come right back here and get in this bed when we're done."

"I think the three orgasms last night and the two today cover whatever you had planned for date four and five."

Crawling up my body, the glint in Tanner's eye is sexy as hell. He takes my lips, and then his stomach growls so loudly, I giggle into his mouth.

"All right, fine. I call uncle. We can leave the bed."

He jumps up and then comes to a halt. I've deprived him of food to the point he's more excited about that than sex.

"Woah, I just got a little lightheaded." He squeezes his eyes shut and wobbles to the side. "Turns out man can't survive on orgasms alone."

I stand and wrap my arms around his neck. "Just out of curiosity, what were date four and five?"

"Date four was renting jet skis and going out on the lake, which we should definitely still do, and date five... involved a lot of candles and wine and a sexy striptease."

"Ooooh, I could get down with the latter," I say and sway my hips.

"Oh no, babe, the striptease is *for* you."

I grab his shirt off the floor and hand it to him. "I'm going to hold you to that, but first let's feed you before you pass out on me." I look around the room for my clothes. "And maybe clean up this place. It stinks like sex and eucalyptus and something else." I take a step and the scent follows me. "Oh no, that third awful smell is me. I need a shower."

"I have an idea. I'll go grab enough food to last us a day or two. We can take turns in the shower, then maybe shower together for good measure, and then we move this party into the other room, and deal with this mess another day." He wags his finger at me. "Tomorrow, though, topless boating lesson."

"That sounds perfect. Everything but the topless part."

He pulls on his T-shirt and then his boxer briefs and jeans. Backing out of the room, he pauses at the doorway.

"What?" I ask when he keeps staring at me with a goofy grin on his face.

"Best date ever. Best *night* ever."

After Tanner leaves, I take a scalding hot shower. I hum as I wash my hair and then my body. I'm in awe of last night and today and how normal it all feels. No, normal isn't even the right word. It feels perfect. We're still us, but in this new fun, very naked way. Everything changed and nothing.

I don't think I've ever been happier or more excited. I know we'll have to leave our little bubble and rejoin the world, but I'm looking forward to another two weeks just like this.

The stink of the room hits me all over again as I walk back into the bedroom.

"Ooof," I say and pull the towel tight around me. I grab my suitcase and roll it over to Tanner's room. I'm starting to run out of clean clothes. Neither of us has bothered to do laundry yet even though the house has a washer and dryer. Another task for another day.

I dig through what remains of my unworn clothes and smile when I get a brilliant outfit idea. Plan in place, I dress and even decide to put on a little makeup. Since I've been at the lake and getting in and out of the water so much, wearing anything other than a swipe of waterproof mascara and lip gloss hasn't made sense.

I've got a perfect wing on my right eye and I'm struggling to get the left to match when there's knocking at the front door. Expecting its Tanner with his hands full of takeout, I take a final look in the mirror, push up my boobs, and hustle out to the living room. The pounding increases in frequency and volume.

"I'm coming, I'm coming," I say as I hurry to the door and fling it open. Hustling in these shoes is not easy. "As good as you imagined?" I ask raising my hands to my side and then immediately regretting all of the life decisions that brought me to this moment. "You're not Tanner," I say to the two wide-eyed girls on my doorstep.

They're both brunette, both staring at me like I'm a crazy person, and both holding overnight bags.

"And you must be Sydney." The taller of the two girls steps by me and enters the house.

The other stands there with her jaw slack. After a few seconds she offers a small smile. "Hi, I'm Corinne."

"Corinne, of course." Which makes the less friendly girl Tara, Tanner's sister. "Come in." I follow her into the living room where the three of us shuffle uncomfortably. "Tanner has told me so much about both of you. He went out to get food, but he should be back any minute. I didn't think you were coming until next week. Does he know you're here?"

"I thought I'd surprise him. Did he take the key out of the plant outside? I couldn't find it."

"Yeah, it's on the counter."

Tara's gaze goes to my feet, and I realize I'm still standing here in front of Tanner's sister in a bikini. "Looks like I succeeded in the surprise part. Cute shoes."

"Oh, right." I lean over and slip out of the pink stilettos and hold them in front of me, hoping they'll shield me from my embarrassment. "You know how it is, have to break them in before you wear them out or they pinch your feet. I'm going to get dressed and let you two get settled."

I walk into Tanner's room with my heart pounding in my chest. Holy fuck. I grab the first article of clothing I find, one of Tanner's gray T-shirts and pull it on along with cutoff shorts. I go for my phone to text Tanner but realize I must have left it in the other room.

"Corinne, you can have my room, I'll take the guest room," Tara says, and I hear footsteps start toward the den of sex.

Oh fuckity fuck fuck.

"Wait!" I call, rushing across the hall just as she steps into the room. Between the condom wrappers and candles and the distinct smell of sex hanging in the air, there's no mistaking what's gone down in here.

"Oh, this is your room?"

"Yeah, I'm sorry. It's a mess. I would have cleaned it already if I knew you were coming. Tanner and I didn't talk about sleeping arrangements when you and your friends got here. Why don't you leave your stuff in the hallway and I'll clean up and move the rest of my stuff to Tanner's room?"

"Oh no, I insist." She backs away like it's a crime scene. "You should stay in here. Corinne and I can share a room."

I'm too mortified to argue or come up with any response except to nod. I can't really blame her for not wanting to stay in here after seeing it in its current state.

When Tanner finally gets back, I'm beyond relieved. He sets the takeout on the counter and then goes to Tara with his arms open. "What are you doing here? I thought you were coming next week?"

She steps into his embrace and they hug. "My professor had a family emergency and moved our classes online for the rest of the summer session. And I wanted to spend an extra few days with my big brother. Eww. You stink, T."

"Uhh... yeah, that was next on the agenda after food." He glances to me. "Did you meet Sydney? I can't believe the two of you haven't met before."

I do a little awkward wave and forced smile.

"I did," Tara says, and she smiles too. "Go shower and then let's take the boat out."

"Sydney and I were going to eat and then stay in tonight."

"It's fine," I say quickly.

"Are you sure?" he asks and all eyes are on me for an answer.

"Absolutely. Who's hungry?"

Tara and Corinne dig into the food while Tanner makes his excuses to shower. I follow him into the bathroom as he strips down. The situation is temporarily forgotten as his body distracts me. Long and lean, muscular in all the right places. He's too good to be true.

"Sorry about our plans." He turns on the shower but then comes back to where I stand in the doorway between the bedroom and bathroom and brushes my hair out of my face. "Make it up to you later?"

"I won't turn that down, but it's fine." Resting my head against his chest, I breathe him in, all the sweat and sex of the past twelve hours. "I opened the door in a bikini and high heels."

His body shakes with laughter around me. "What?"

"I was going to surprise you with my orange bikini and pink heels, but instead, I gave your sister and her friend an eyeful. And then she walked into our sex headquarters. I can't imagine what she must think of me."

"She's not some young innocent."

"Still, that was not the first impression I was hoping for."

"We'll go out on the boat and then come back and spend the night on the patio hanging out. You two can chat and get to know one another."

I nod and he moves to the shower. "Are you coming in?"

"No, I think I'll go eat with them." Maybe I shouldn't care if Tara knows we're in here showering together, but I feel like she's learned enough about her brother's sex life for one day.

Tara sits in the seat across from Tanner on the boat as he drives us around the lake. I pull my feet up and hug my knees and watch the easy way they interact. They have the same straight nose and a lot of the same facial expressions. The way they smile—small at first and then widening. And the way they hold their mouths when they talk.

Tanner's hair is darker than his sister's and her eyes aren't as deep blue. She's pretty and I think she's nice despite not seeming to want anything to do with me. We've barely spoken, and I get the feeling she wishes I were anywhere but here though I'm not sure why. Maybe she was hoping to spend some quality time with Tanner alone. Although she brought Corinne, so I don't think that's it.

A night of drinking on the patio and I'm sure we can fix whatever it is. For now, I'm content to sit back and let the two of them catch up.

I'm in my own little world as Tara tells him about school and people I don't know. There's something so peaceful and relaxing about being out on the lake that I can feel it easing my worries. It's the change in Tanner's tone that snaps me out of my serene moment.

"I told you that's over," he says, and his shoulders stiffen.

"But you didn't say why, and Amelia won't say a word either. She seemed so good for you. You can't keep breaking up with girls every time you get bored or things get hard. Relationships take work."

"I know... that's not..." He glances over his shoulder and I'm quick to lookout into the water to give them the illusion of privacy. "It doesn't matter. Sydney and I are together now, so you can stop worrying about me dying a single bachelor. I swear you're worse than mom and grandma combined."

Chapter Twenty-One

TANNER

"Do you want another drink, babe?" I ask as I scoot back my chair.

"No, I'm good." Her voice is deep and husky. She's tired as hell but being a trooper to hang out with my sister.

Corinne went to bed an hour ago, but Tara is still drinking and chatting with no end in sight. I don't get to see her as often as I'd like, so I suck up my own tiredness and grab two more beers from the fridge.

Sydney's curled up, arms wrapped around her bare calves and face tilted resting on her shoulder. Tara's staring down at her phone.

"Here you go." I place one of the beers in front of Tara and then take a seat. "Last one for me. I'm beat."

"I think I'm going to go to bed now," Sydney says. She smiles apologetically to Tara. "It's really great to finally meet you. I hope we can hang out more over the next week, after I've slept."

Tara sets her phone on the table and wraps her fingers around the neck of the beer. "You too."

I stand as Sydney does and place a kiss on her lips. "I'll be there soon."

Sydney nods and glances at Tara. "'Night."

She slips inside the house and I drop back into my seat at the table.

"So, what else is new?" I ask.

"No, no. We're talking about you."

"You already know everything. I still haven't made a decision about next year, so if Mom and Dad sent you to get answers, you're not going to get any. Or maybe it's your own initiative—annoy me into doing what you think is best."

"Well, I am curious about where your head's at, but I promise I'm here only for the lake. And, seriously, give me a little credit," she huffs. "I'd never do Mom and Dad's bidding."

"Sorry, I know. I got an email from Coach Wiles yesterday. He wants to set a meeting for when I get back to Valley."

"About what?"

"If I had to guess, he found out I'm considering quitting baseball to focus on basketball."

"Are you though?"

I squirm in my seat, not wanting to think about it, let alone talk about it. "I don't know."

"You'll figure it out, T, and Mom and Dad will be fine with whatever you decide. Has Dad been calling and asking you?"

"Not since I left Valley. I told him I wanted the summer to decide and he's respected that."

"They just want to feel involved."

With a sigh, I sit back in my chair. "Yeah."

"What's the plan for the Fourth?" she asks. "I invited so many people I'm not sure how we're going to fit them if they all show up."

"I have an idea about that actually. What if we had the party at Jonah's? He's got more room and that killer pool."

"He'd be okay with that?"

"Yeah, he already mentioned it. We'll help him pitch in for booze and whatever else he needs."

"Mom and Dad really should have bought a house with a pool."

"The pool is right there," I deepen my voice to mock my dad and motion to the lake.

"And it's free to heat," we say together and then laugh.

"I missed you, T," Tara says.

"Missed you too. I'm glad you came down early. We can hang out more and you can get to know Sydney."

"No offense, but spending quality time with your fuck buddy is not what I had in mind for my extra week at the lake."

I scrunch up my face at the phrase coming out of my baby sister's mouth. "Fuck buddy? Seriously?"

"Oh, I'm sorry, your *best friend*." She air quotes the last two words and then rolls her eyes. "It's no wonder you can't keep a girlfriend. Amelia was worried about her, seems with good reason."

"Okay, pump the breaks. Sydney was my best friend. She still is, but we decided we wanted more. And I plan on keeping this one, so stop stressing."

"You two are really together then? A couple?"

"Yeah." I chuckle. I swear I couldn't convince people we were just friends and now they don't want to believe we're more than that. "We're really together."

"I don't get it. I'm sorry. I don't. I think it's entirely too convenient you finally get together when it's only the two of you out here at the lake. Why now? What's different?"

"You're analyzing it way too hard." I laugh it off but worries I hadn't even considered cross my mind and there's a pit in my stomach that wasn't there a minute ago. Things are different now, aren't they? Or are we screwing up our friendship by giving in to the chemistry between us?

"I don't want to see you get hurt and it seems like every time you get serious with someone else it ends because of your friendship with Sydney."

"You don't know what you're talking about."

"Why did things end with Amelia?" she asks pointedly.

"Aaaaand, I'm going to bed. See you in the morning, Tara."

Inside, I toss my beer in the recycling and head to my room. Sydney's not in my bed so I go across the hall and crack the door. It's dark, but I can tell it's her.

I kick off my shoes and undress then slide onto the mattress in front of her. Dark lashes flutter and then open and slowly her lips pull into a smile.

"Hey." She nuzzles into me and I wrap my arms around her so I can pull her close against me.

This is what's different. This feeling when we're together. A completeness I've never felt before. Being best friends with Sydney was great, but being her boyfriend is everything. Maybe it took us getting away from Valley to figure it out, but we were always inevitable. I knew it before I ever admitted it to myself.

"I'm glad you're here," I whisper against her skin.

She hums her agreement and snuggles closer and her breathing evens out immediately.

The next morning I wake up to an empty bed. It still smells like sex in this room which makes me grin and also wish Sydney hadn't already left. I pull on my jeans and head out to find her.

Tara and Corinne are on the deck in their suits, but I find Sydney sorting clothes and putting them into the washing machine.

"We need to have a serious conversation about waking up so early." I drop a kiss to her shoulder.

"It's after ten."

"Really? Fuck, I'm surprised Tara let me sleep in so long."

"I think you had about fifteen more minutes before her patience ran out."

"Tanner, fucking finally!" my sister screeches as she shuts the sliding door behind her. "Get dressed, let's go!"

I back out of the room and pull Sydney with me. "Five minutes. Twenty tops. Pack the cooler while we get ready."

Sydney yelps and her cheeks pink as I drag her toward the bedroom. Tara rolls her eyes. "You have twelve and then I'm leaving you behind."

I know she won't. She hates docking the boat. Plus, she wants to hang out with me too much.

"Why do you look so embarrassed, babe?" I ask once we're in the bathroom and I start undressing.

"Your sister knows we're in here to..." She bobs her head. "You know."

"Have sex?" I bite back a smile as I push my jeans down and my dick springs up.

Sydney slaps my chest playfully. "I want her to like me."

"She does. She will. Tara's a little guarded. You just need to spend more time together." I link my arms behind her back. "A day out on the lake, and a cooler of beer is all you need. Well, that, and a couple of orgasms beforehand."

Her gaze doesn't even drop to my penis. "I'm going to help them pack the cooler."

"One night of sex and I'm already cast aside." I sigh, loud and dramatic. It doesn't work. She leaves me holding my dick.

Jonah texts as we're preparing to head down to the water, and we decide to head to his place to hang out for the day, instead.

"Jonah, hey," Tara says with a big grin and hurries off the boat and to him.

"Missed you T. Shaw." He wraps her into a bear hug and lifts her off the ground.

"Have your biceps gotten bigger?" she asks and makes a big show of wrapping both hands around his right arm.

I shake my head. Just what Jonah needs, someone stroking his ego.

Tara and Jonah take out the jet skis and the rest of us set up a giant raft on the lake. Tara's a daredevil zipping along the water ahead of Jonah. Corinne is pretty much her polar opposite, but I guess that's why they've been friends so long. Ollie and my sister's reserved friend go up to the pool leaving me and Sydney to ourselves.

It's another perfect day with my favorite person sprawled out next to me, a beer in hand, the sun high in the sky.

"Have Tara and Jonah hung out a lot?" Sydney asks, and I follow her line of sight where they sit dead in the water. My sister's head is thrown back and even from fifty yards her laughter carries.

"Nah, not really. A couple of times when she's come down over the summer."

"I don't think she likes me very much." Sydney smooths a hand over the flyaway hairs that have escaped from her ponytail.

"She's just salty about Amelia."

"What do you mean?"

"Tara liked her. They met that weekend Amelia went home with me and they've kept in touch."

"I don't understand why that would make her dislike me."

I rub a hand over my jaw. "Tara thinks that you're the reason Amelia and I broke up."

"Why would she think that? You told her Amelia broke up with you, right? Wait, Amelia *did* break up with you, didn't she?"

I hesitate.

"Tanner?" Sydney's voice lifts and her brown eyes widen. "You told me Amelia broke up with you."

"She did. That was true."

"Because of me?" Her brown eyes press me for the truth.

"She said I was in love with you. Actually, first she said you were in love with me but then when I told her how you were trying to help me smooth things over she changed her mind and said I was the one in love with you."

Sydney sits up on the raft and she regards me carefully. "And what did you say?"

"Nothing. I left."

"So it really was my fault that you and Amelia broke up." Sydney looks thrown by the new information and I scramble to console her.

"No, babe, it was mine. It's on me, not you. Tara thinks I'm going to ruin every relationship because I cut and run at the first sign of conflict."

"And I'm who you run back to."

I nod.

"Do you think you could have worked things out with Amelia if you'd stayed and tried to talk it out?"

"Maybe."

Sydney groans. "And we never would have gotten together."

I take her hands in my lap. "Babe, this has been the best couple of weeks. I wouldn't change it for anything."

"Me either." Even though she's reaffirming how great a time we've been having, her tone isn't nearly as excited.

When Jonah and Tara make it back, Corinne's already red from the sun and complaining she needs a nap.

"What? No way. It's still early," Ollie whines.

"I need to go into town this afternoon for physical therapy anyway," Sydney says, and I know she's trying to make Corinne feel better for us all going back.

"Tomorrow let's hook up the tube and have some fun," Jonah suggests before we leave.

Corinne falls asleep on the ride back, Tara's on her phone, and Sydney is quiet—very unlike her usual bubbly self. I know she's stressing about my sister liking her.

My instinct is to ignore it and let them come together on their own. Sydney is impossible not to like when you get to know her, so I have no doubt my sister will come around eventually. But maybe a little push would help resolve things quicker.

Corinne wakes up just long enough to walk up to the house and fall into bed. I'm sitting in the living room while my sister and my girl are on their separate sides of the house showering.

Sydney comes out first. Her long hair is still wet and hangs straight over her shoulders.

She smiles and walks over to me and I pull her down on my lap.

"You smell good."

"You smell like the lake." She nuzzles into me regardless.

"Don't worry, I'm going to shower while you're gone. Then it's you and me for date four."

"Jet skis?" She perks up.

"Yep, Jonah offered to let us use them tonight if you're game."

"That sounds amazing."

"Well, I can't find my contact solution," Tara announces as she walks into the living room wearing her glasses. "And I completely forgot to pack underwear."

"Ugh," I groan at the overshare.

"Relax, I'm wearing my suit bottoms."

Sydney sits tall on my lap. "I'm going into town if you want me to pick up some? Contact solution that is, not underwear."

"Oh, no, that's okay. I can get it tomorrow or the next day." Tara waves her off.

"Go together," I suggest.

Both girls look to me. "You both need to go to town, and I know neither of you like to shop alone." I shrug. "Corinne and I will hold down the fort with our napping while you're gone."

They don't speak, so I stand setting Sydney on the floor. "Cool, it's settled. I'll grill when you guys get back."

Chapter Twenty-Two

SYDNEY

I rub my palms along my thighs. "Thanks for driving. I hate taking Tanner's Firebird out. Knowing how much he loves it makes me nervous and I end up driving like fifteen miles an hour."

"It's no problem."

It's just me and Tara and Luke Bryan on the radio. She makes me more nervous than I am when driving Tanner's precious car and I have to resist my natural tendency to babble. But I can't just sit here mute either.

"Do you like country music?"

"Yeah, Tanner teases me about it constantly." She turns the station before I can tell her I actually don't mind it

"Like he's one to talk. I found two songs by 98° on one of his Spotify playlists. And what's with his obsession with Sinatra?"

"Oh, I know! His musical taste is all over the map and some of it is just strange. Every Christmas we have to listen to the Rat Pack Christmas album on repeat while we put up the tree." Tara laughs and we share a commiserating glance before her smile falls and she returns her stare out the windshield.

It feels as if every time I make a crack in her defenses, she's quick to slam the guard back up. Like she doesn't want to like me. Tanner said she only met Amelia the once so I can't figure out why Tara is so salty about me allegedly breaking them up. Let's say it is all my fault, why does that make her hate me?

Amelia is nice, but she's not so nice that I should be treated as the bitch by comparison.

But, I am nothing if not determined to make Tara like me.

"I'm really glad you came down early. I've been dying to meet you. Tanner talks about you so fondly."

No response just a polite nod.

"Anyway, I'm glad. I'm crazy about him and I know things are new, but—"

"Look, Sydney," she interrupts. "I know that you and my brother are close and I get why you'd get together when he's single again and it's just the two of you alone at the lake, but you don't have to pretend that it's more than what it is. I know Tanner. He bounces from girl to girl, and he's out at the first sign of trouble. You two have sort of a pattern, picking up every time he's single. The point is, we don't have to act like you two are more than fuck buddies."

A shocked squeak is all I'm capable of before she stops outside of the physical therapy office. I get the first semi-genuine smile since I've met her as she says, "Pick you up in an hour?"

"She sounds like a bitch." Emily's indignant tone is everything I could want in a best friend. Especially one I kept in the dark about Tanner and me until five minutes ago. Regardless, she always has my back and is ready to make me feel better about anyone who does me wrong. Unfortunately, right now, I don't want to hate on the person who made me feel like shit.

"The thing is, I don't think she is. She's nice to everyone else, and there are these moments where she lets her guard down and I feel like we could be friends." I sit on the dock near the water's edge. "Or at least civil. I can't believe she called me his fuck buddy."

"What does Tanner say?" I glance up at the house where he's grilling while Tara and Corinne sit at the outdoor table drinking and chatting.

"Not much. It's his sister, Em, what am I supposed to do?"

"I don't know, but do not let her treat you like shit. I'll be there in a few days and I'll happily tell her to go fuck herself if she hasn't come over to the bright side by then."

"The bright side?"

"The Sydney side. You're amazing and colorful, full of life. So, yes, the bright side."

"I can't wait to see you." I smile, holding the phone to my ear. "All right. I should go. We're having dinner and then Tanner and I are going out."

"Okay. Have fun. Enjoy the time with your man and forget about Tara."

I wish that last part was as easy as the first. Tanner and I have no problem enjoying ourselves. We never have.

After we take the jet skis around the lake, we take the boat to his favorite spot and jump in the water. He rests on a floatie and I wrap myself around him.

"I love being out here at night." I tip my head back and look up into the dark sky. "It feels like it's our own personal lake."

"Someday we can build a house right over there." His lips find my shoulder and one hand lifts from the water to point to an unbuilt area between two houses. They set far enough back from the water that the spot still feels private.

"A lot of assumptions in that statement."

He chuckles softly. "You don't think the land is for sale?"

"That was at the bottom of my concerns."

"Well, you're stuck with me and I'm going to have a place here someday, so pick your spot."

"Stuck with you, huh?"

"Like glue."

"I don't need glue. That should be obvious after two years." I swallow thickly. "Even if things didn't work out between us as a couple, I'd still want you in my life."

"Same, babe. We need those best friends forever necklaces where we each get half a heart."

"I am not wearing BFF necklaces with you."

"Matching tattoos?"

I groan. "That's like the kiss of death for any relationship."

"I'm going to think of something," he says. "Some symbolic way to show the whole world we're two peas in a pod. Peas in a pod... maybe there's something there."

Shaking my head, I can't help but laugh. "You're the least sentimental and symbolic person I know."

His jaw drops.

"Don't even pretend to be offended. You throw away every birthday card and handwritten letter, photos..."

"It's just stuff. Doesn't mean I don't appreciate the sentiment."

"I suppose."

As we go quiet, I'm lost in my own thoughts about his sister and everything she said. I want to ask him what will happen with us when we get back to Valley, but I can't bring myself to ask. Before Tara mentioned it, I hadn't thought of myself as a rebound, but is that what I've been? Not just this time, but always?

Not that we hooked up or any of that before, but after every breakup, we always spend more time together. Each time I wondered if it would be the time that something might happen between us. I tried not to acknowledge the thoughts, but they were there.

Now that it's happened, I have to wonder, am I Tanner's fall back girl? Would we have ever gotten together if we hadn't been alone together at the lake?

I know that he would never use me like that on purpose, and if I voiced my worries, he'd probably have something reassuring to say to ease my mind, but I don't want to ruin what's left of his time here at the lake. He already has a lot on his plate he's trying to avoid. Two more weeks of his last carefree summer. I'd have to be a monster to wreck that.

And maybe I want to enjoy these last carefree moments with him without risking it blowing up in my face.

"Let's go up on the boat." I glide my hands over his abs and wriggle against his crotch.

"Don't have to ask me twice." He swims with me attached to his front. I let go when we reach the ladder and hurry up. Tanner's right behind me and swoops me up. He sits on the bench in the back of the boat with me on his lap.

Goose bumps pop up along my arms and legs from the chill of the night air on my wet skin. Tanner runs his calloused palms up my back. He cradles my neck with one hand and the other travels down to my hip and slides under the fabric of my bikini bottoms.

His mouth takes mine and his tongue demands entrance

immediately. The warmth of his mouth and the friction of our bodies pressed together chases the chill.

The gentle sway of the boat does a lot of the work for us, brushing my center against his. Tanner's lips move down my face to my neck and then my chest. He kisses my exposed flesh and then his hot suction covers my nipple through the spandex material.

With a little maneuvering, I untie his trunks and push my hand inside. His dick is deliciously hard, and he lifts his hips allowing me better access. I wrap my fingers around him and stroke gently until he groans.

"Babe, I don't have a condom."

"I'm on the pill..." I stop. "But that's okay, we don't have to have sex. I can be creative."

I have every intention of getting to my knees, but he pumps into my hand.

"Thank fuck. I didn't want to ask, but I've been thinking about being inside of you without a condom. I've never slept bare with anyone."

I've seen his stash of condoms back at Valley, so I believe him.

His thumb circles my clit and then one long finger slides under the material and pushes it to the side. I shift and he guides his dick into me slowly. At this angle he fills me so completely. I hadn't expected it to feel different for me without a condom, but it does. I close my eyes and enjoy every sensation before slowly moving.

"So good," he says as he nips at my neck and collarbone. "You feel incredible. Hot, wet, fucking amazing."

His hands roam all over my body and settle on the curve of my waist. He lets me set the pace even though I can tell he wants me to move faster. I'm enjoying it too much. I don't want to rush it. Just us on the boat, nothing around, nothing between us—it's perfect and I want to hold on to this perfection before I go back to worrying about all the stupid things trying to make me forget why it's worth the risk.

The next two days, Tara and Corinne go out on their own more than they hang with us, which honestly is fine by me. It feels like good fortune to escape with Tanner back into our little bubble.

My good luck runs out on the day Emily is set to arrive. A downpour of rain that starts in the early morning continues on and off into the afternoon.

Tanner and I are snuggled up on the couch while Tara and Corinne are in the kitchen baking cookies that smell amazing but are probably laced with her disapproval and contempt for me.

I'm looking forward to Emily getting here so that I'll have someone to talk to. If Tanner has noticed the lingering weirdness between me and Tara, he hasn't mentioned it., and I haven't brought it up again. How do you tell your boyfriend that his sister called you his fuck buddy anyway? And even if I told him, what could he do? He might talk to her and then she'd just dislike me even more. I think I'm going to have to accept that Tanner's sister may never like me. I hope he's okay with that. I get an awful feeling when I try to picture holidays together or meeting his parents. Can we really make a relationship work when someone so close to him dislikes me?

"What time is Emily getting here?" Tanner asks. "Going out on the boat is probably out but we could take her to The Cove."

A knock at the door gets all our attention.

"Guess that answers that." He stands. "I'm going to jump in the shower while you two catch up."

I hurry to the door and fling it open with a big smile, but come up short when it isn't my best friend on the other side, but Tanner's ex.

"Amelia?"

"Sydney?" She glances around as if she might be at the wrong house. "Is Tanner here?"

"Yeah, of course, come in." I manage to be polite despite my shock.

Amelia gives a small, awkward wave when she sees Tara and Corinne. "Hey."

"Oh my gosh, you came!" Tara comes forward and hugs her like they're long lost best friends.

My eyes prick with tears. "I'll get Tanner for you."

I keep my head down as I walk through the living room and toward the bedroom. Tanner's pulling his T-shirt over his head and starts to smile, but then pauses.

"What's wrong?"

"Amelia is here." My voice sounds weak even to my own ears.

"Amelia?" he asks as he goes to the door and looks out. His brows pull together. "Be right back."

Sitting on the bed, I let out a shaky breath. I can't make out exactly what they say, but I can tell from their tone and exchange that Tanner's as surprised that she's here as I am. I have a choice. I can sit in here and hide until she's gone, or I can go out there and sit beside my man.

As I step out, Tanner is pulling back from an awkward hug. "What are you doing here?"

Amelia glances over to where Tara stands nearby in her apron. "Tara invited me, but I was hoping we could talk?"

Tanner's jaw flexes as he looks to his sister. "Of course, come on. Let's go outside it looks like the rain's let up."

I don't realize I'm holding my breath until the sliding door shuts Tanner and Amelia on the other side. White hot anger and frustration bubbles to the surface.

"*You* invited Amelia?" Crossing my arms, I face off with Tara.

"I called to tell her that I thought she and Tanner should sit down and really talk about their breakup. It isn't what either of them really wanted, but they were both being stubborn." She goes back to the kitchen. "She was supposed to come down this week anyway."

"That was before they broke up."

She shrugs as if it's no big deal.

"Do you really not see how fucked-up this is?"

"If it's really over between them than what does it matter? She'll get closure and Tanner will come crawling back to you like he always does."

"That is not... he doesn't..." I stop. "I don't owe you any explanation." I turn on my heel to go wait for Tanner in the bedroom before I say something I regret.

"If you care about him, like you claim to, then you'll give him a chance to be happy," Tara says to my back.

I face her prepared to tell her to go to hell, but I can't do that. She's Tanner's sister, and even if I want to punch her, I won't do anything to hurt Tanner.

"Do you really think that's ever going to be possible with the two of you carrying on?" she asks. "No girl is ever going to accept your relationship with him. I've watched helplessly over the past two years while he blew it with every girl that he met." She walks toward me. "He'd call and tell me about some new girl he was dating, and then slowly he'd ruin each one. They'd get jealous of the time he spent with you and then figure out he was cheating on them with you. And all it took was the slightest hint of conflict and Tanner was all too eager to bail. Why have a girlfriend that makes you work for it when you have a best friend that's always around? You've ruined every relationship he's had since he met you."

Her words hurt but I try not to show it. "You don't know what you're talking about."

"Maybe not, but tell me, do you really think you and Tanner would be together now if you hadn't screwed things up with him and Amelia?" She gives me her back before I can respond, and I rush into the bedroom before the tears stinging my eyes have a chance to fall.

She's wrong. She has no idea what she's talking about. So why do I feel so awful?

Chapter Twenty-Three

TANNER

"Tara asked you to come?"

Amelia rests her clasped hands in her lap and nods tenta-tively. "Please don't be mad at her for meddling. The truth is I was looking for any excuse to come."

"I'm sorry. I'm a little thrown off here." Understatement of the year. Why the hell would Tara call Amelia and invite her down? We broke up.

Amelia explains how Tara called and voiced her opinion that I wasn't really over her and I was just avoiding conflict. Opinion because that's not even close to accurate.

"So, I jumped into the car and here I am." Her shoulders fall and she lets out a long breath.

"I do hate conflict." I chuckle. "But the reason I didn't call is because I realized you were right."

Her tight smile drops into a line. "You said you were just friends?"

"We were."

"But now you're together?" The implication is there even if

she doesn't come right out and ask if I cheated or knowingly dated her while secretly pining for my best friend.

"I'm sorry if I ever made you doubt how much I cared about you. I did. I still do."

"I should have called. Driving down was a little spontaneous, but I had to know for sure."

"I could have saved you a trip."

"It's really over then? There's no chance we could try again?"

My aversion to conflict rears its head, and I squirm as I realize I have to break up with this great girl in front of me. Because of course Amelia is great, she's just not the one for me. If closure is what she came here for, then I can give her that at least.

"You're amazing, Amelia. I had a lot of fun with you, but you were right. I didn't even realize how right you were. You knew I was in love with Sydney before I did." I offer her a sheepish grin.

"I didn't want to believe it. I know I said it, but I hoped I was wrong, and you'd call. Maybe I didn't want to admit she was better for you than me."

"How do you mean?"

"You're different with her. You smile and laugh a lot more. I hoped it was just friendship, but I guess I always knew. You have all these inside jokes, and you're always competing over silly things. She gets you in a way no one else does. It's the reason I could never hate her even when I really wanted to. You two are perfect together." She lets out an audible sigh and looks up to the sky as the rain starts back up. "I should go."

"I'm really sorry." It doesn't escape me that I'm apologizing for something I couldn't control, nor would I have even if I'd known, but I am sorry that it hurt Amelia in the process.

We stand and I hug her goodbye and then walk her back into the house and to the front door. The living room and kitchen are mysteriously vacant. I figured my sister would have her ear to the door. I still can't believe she called Amelia. Tara's never been shy about voicing her opinions, but she's never done anything like this before.

The light in her room is on. She looks up from where she lies on her stomach on top of the bed. "Hey."

"Hey?" I arch a brow and lean against the doorframe. Corinne sits on the floor folding clothes but avoids eye contact. "What the hell was that?"

"Look, Tanner, I love you, but you keep missing what's right in front of you."

My thoughts go to Sydney, but I don't think that's what she means.

"You're going to have to break it down for me then because the only thing I can see is how fucked-up it is that you invited my ex-girlfriend down to the same house my current girlfriend is staying." I glance back out into the living room. "Where is Sydney anyway?"

"She left."

"What? Why?" I pull out my phone to see if she texted. It isn't like her to just leave. Yeah, it might be awkward that my ex showed up, but Sydney knows I'd never get back with Amelia. At least I think she does.

Tara meets my gaze and then hers flits away.

"What's that face?" It hits me slowly. Guilty as hell, that's what that face is. "Tara, what did you say to her?"

"I was honest. Maybe a little too honest, but she needed to hear it." Tara gets to her feet. "Sydney seems nice enough and she's beautiful, of course, but, come on, she's not the girl for you long-term."

"What the hell are you talking about?"

"You keep ruining perfectly good relationships. Amelia is just the last in a long line. I thought if you talked to her you could work things out. You seemed to really like this one, and I liked her too. Don't blow it because you want to live in this casual fun lifestyle forever. I see guys do it at my school all the time. There are all these great girls, but they continually sleep around with whichever girl hangs around the most."

"I don't have enough time to tell you all the ways you're wrong. Sydney isn't some girl who's been hanging around for two years happy to fill in the gaps between girlfriends. She's my best friend and I love her. I've been in love with her. So, whatever grand scheme you concocted to parade all my ex-girlfriends in here and try to help me get over my relationship issues and chase Sydney away, know this: I choose Sydney. I've chosen her a million times, and I'll do it a million times more." I'm so pissed, but I can deal with Tara later. "I need to find my girl."

I check the bedrooms just in case, but there's no sign of Sydney. After grabbing my keys from the kitchen, I rush to the door.

"Tanner?" Corinne calls out.

I throw open the door but pause.

"I overheard her on the phone. I think she's heading back to Valley."

"Thank you."

Sprinting through the rain, I make it to my car and hop in before I realize Amelia hasn't left. She's sitting in her car watching the rain pelt down.

Shit.

I hop back out and run to her car. Big, cold drops drench my T-shirt.

She rolls the window down an inch. "I'm just waiting for it to let up."

As dark as the sky is, she might be waiting awhile.

"Wait inside."

"Oh no, it's okay."

"Amelia, it's fine. I'm going to find Sydney, but we'll be back."

She doesn't make any move to turn off the car and I continue to get soaked while trying to convince her.

"Please? I'll feel better knowing you're not trying to drive in this."

"All right. You're sure?" she asks.

"Positive."

Thankfully she turns off the car and I run her back to the house before I can go about my original mission. Find Sydney and kiss her until she realizes she's the only girl for me.

Chapter Twenty-Four

SYDNEY

"The things she said, Em." I swipe a hand over both sides of my cheek to collect the tears I can't seem to stop. "She made what Tanner and I have feel so... wrong. Am I the reason all his relationships end? Is he only with me because I've gotten in the way so many times? Have I made myself the only option by chasing them all away?" I could maybe stand his sister's wrath, but the idea that I might have somehow been responsible for hurting Tanner makes me feel sick.

I close my eyes and avoid meeting the gaze of Allyson, the Uber driver who keeps sending pitying looks into the rearview mirror.

"I swear to God I'm gonna have to pull this car over, I'm shaking with anger." Emily's tone is sharp as nails. God, I love her.

"Where are you? Did you turn back? I wouldn't blame you between the weather and my drama."

"No freaking way. I'm still coming. I'm going to tell that wench what I think of her and maybe slap Tanner over the head for good measure. I may have to pull over though, the rain's starting to come down harder again and between that and my rage I'm not seeing that great."

"He didn't know," I tell her. "I could see the shock on his face when Amelia showed up."

"Then why are you running?"

"I'm not running. Allyson and I are driving around while I figure out what to do."

"Allyson?"

"My Uber driver." I briefly meet her gaze in the mirror and smile awkwardly.

"You ran," she says decisively. "Though I'm not sure I understand why. You didn't do anything wrong."

"Because some part of me wonders if Tara's right. Maybe Tanner and I had our shot two years ago, and I should have bowed out and let him move on."

"You don't really believe that. You can't. Whether or not you two work as a couple, it doesn't change what you've meant to each other over the years. Don't let her ugly view of it, tarnish yours."

I think back on our friendship. The fun times we've had are the first to come to mind, but that's not all it's been. Tanner and I have seen each other through hard times too. I don't know why I'm so quick to discredit what I've been to him when, if it's anything like what he's been to me, means so much more than anyone else could understand.

"Crap," I mutter under my breath and sit forward.

"Uh-oh. What now?"

"I've got to go back."

"That a girl! Don't let Tara, or anyone else, speak for Tanner. Keep me posted. I'm stopping at the next exit to eat and wait out the storm. Go get your man."

I drop my phone and lean forward. "Allyson, I—"

"On it." She pulls a sharp U-turn that sends me back against my seat. The rain has definitely picked up here and traffic is slow.

My phone buzzes next to me. Tanner's name lights up my screen with a text, **Babe, where are you?**

He's called a half-dozen times, but I needed to clear my head before I talked to him. Can I really tell him why I left? I don't know what to do, but I can't believe I was stupid enough to leave. Who's the one avoiding conflict now? I don't respond. I'll know what to say when I see him. Or at least that's my hope.

"Good luck," Allyson says as she pulls up in front of the house.

"Thank you." I hurry out of the car. A heavy sheet of rain makes it nearly impossible to see more than a foot in front of me. I navigate to the front door and shake off under the overhang. I'm positive I look a mess, but I'm back and I'm not leaving until Tanner knows exactly what he means to me.

I'm not sure what scene I expected to walk into, but Tara, Corinne, and Amelia sitting together in the living room was not it. Tara has the gall to look surprised I'm back.

I bypass them completely and hurry to the bedroom.

"Where is Tanner?" I ask as I backtrack to the living room. I'm dripping on the floor and the blast of air conditioning makes me shiver.

"He went after you," Tara says dryly.

"After me where?"

"We thought you went back to Valley," Corinne says.

I groan at my own stupidity for sending him on a freaking rat race and pull out my phone. The last time he called, Tanner left a message. I listen as I turn my back to the girls.

"Babe, I'm so sorry. I don't know what all Tara said to

you, but she was wrong. Everyone's wrong. Amelia and I are over. I've been thinking over the past few weeks how no one really understands us. When we were friends, people wanted us to be more, and when we finally gave in, that seemed to confuse people too. It doesn't confuse me. You're not one thing. You're everything. You're my best friend and you're my girlfriend. You're the only person who really sees me for exactly who I am." There's a pause and then he adds, "Call me back."

Tears blur my vision and I laugh out of relief and happiness as I fumble to call him back. He put something to words I've never been able to. We've never fit into a tidy category and we never will because we're so much more than that.

He answers on the first ring. "Hey, where are you?"

"I'm at the house. I didn't go back to Valley. I'm here." The lights flicker.

"Thank god you're safe. Stay there. Tell everyone to stay put. It's getting really nasty out here. My phone is about to die, and I don't have my charger, but I'm headed back."

"Okay, I'll tell them."

So many things that I want to say, but his tone is distracted and serious as he navigates the storm. "Be careful. I'll see you when you get here."

"Yep, I will. See you soon."

"Bye." I keep the phone to my ear as I face the three other women in the house. The lights flicker again and then stay off. While it's cloudy outside, there's enough light coming in through the windows that I can still see their questioning stares. "He's on his way back, and he said we should all stay put because of the crappy driving conditions."

Corinne gets up and tries flipping the light switch a few times before she says, "Looks like the power is out."

"I'm sure it'll be back soon," Tara says. "I'm going to paint my nails."

Corinne follows Tara, leaving me and Amelia alone.

"I'm just waiting for the storm to pass and then I'm going," Amelia says, looking as pumped as I am about being trapped together. "I'm sorry that I showed up unannounced. I didn't know you were here. Though I should have."

Amelia and I have always gotten along, but we're not exactly friends. When she was dating Tanner, I went out of my way to make her feel comfortable, but I never really felt like she believed I wasn't out to steal her man.

I realize it probably seems like that's exactly what I did, given how things turned out.

"I get it. Tanner's great. I would have done the same thing if I were in your position."

"Yeah, I see that. Next time, we should remember to take an umbrella." Her laugh is brittle.

I glance down at my wet T-shirt and shorts. And that's the difference between us. I don't need an umbrella. Probably would have tossed one if I'd had it because it would have slowed me down. Some people are worth running through the rain for.

"I should get changed." I offer her a small smile.

The master bedroom is darker than the living room with its big windows and sliding door. I strip out of my clothes and towel off. After I'm dressed, I sit on the bed to avoid going back out there.

I text Emily to let her know the power is out and the roads are dicey to which she replies that she's going to head back home. I was really looking forward to seeing her and a distraction would be good about now.

Holding my phone in hand, I stare at the dark screen and

will Tanner to get here. I didn't ask how far away he was, so I don't know if soon is five minutes or twenty.

At the thirty mark, also known as the brink of insanity, I wander back out. Amelia's moved to the window and looks out. Tara and Corinne lie on the floor with their phones and half a dozen nail polish bottles.

"You should save your battery in case the power stays out," I say.

"Eh, I'm sure it'll be back soon. It went out last summer for like an hour." Tara doesn't look up as she blows off my suggestion.

Ignoring her, I move to stand by the counter in the kitchen. I'm too anxious to sit. I feel uneasy and I'm not sure if it's only because I'm in a room with my boyfriend's ex and his psycho sister. My fingers curl around my phone. I want to call him and see where he is, make sure he's safe, but I don't want him to answer or run his battery down if he's on his way. I just need to know he's all right.

After an hour, Tara finally looks concerned. "Maybe he pulled off to wait out the worst of it." Her brow furrows as she glances out. The rain has slowed, but the wind still blows hard and the thunder continues. "I'm going to call him."

An unsettled feeling spreads through me and I pace and bring my thumbnail to my mouth while Tara holds the phone to her ear for long enough that I know Tanner isn't answering.

"Straight to voicemail," she says, ends the call, and tries again.

"His phone probably died."

"Should we go try to find him? What if he's had an accident?"

"Let's not assume the worst," I say, even though I'm

currently swiping through a mental slideshow of all kinds of horrendous possibilities.

"We can't just leave him out there," Tara insists.

"He said to stay put." I want to be here about as much as I want to stab a sharp stick into my eye, but panicking isn't going to help.

Tara rolls her eyes, but I find an unlikely advocate in Corinne who says, "Sydney's probably right. Let's not do anything rash just yet."

"I'm going to find my brother," Tara says as she heads to the door. "I can't just sit here and—"

"There's a tree down on the highway," Amelia interrupts. "It's shut down in both directions."

A heavy silence settles around us and the pit in my stomach grows until I want to double over in pain.

"Where would he go if he couldn't get here?" I ask.

"Jonah's maybe?" There's genuine worry on Tara's face that temporarily makes me forget how awful she is.

"That's thirty minutes by road in good weather." The thought of him out there stranded makes my stomach drop. "I'll text Jonah."

Keeping myself busy edges away a little of the dread, but as I scroll through my phone, I realize I don't have Jonah's number.

"Crap, I don't have it. Do you?"

Tara shakes her head. "No, but maybe I have someone else in my contacts."

"Good thinking," I say, thinking of Datson. "I'll check mine too."

The power of four girls and the contacts in their phones is impressive, but nearly an hour later, we've exhausted them all and no one has heard from Tanner.

"And now my phone is dead," Tara says with a groan.

"I'm at five percent," Corinne adds.

"Seven." Amelia slides hers onto the coffee table.

As I'm deciding whether or not it's too extreme to call the highway patrol or hospitals, I'm struck with an idea. "Is there some sort of online social media group for the neighborhood or a local highway patrol page we could check for updates on accidents and road closures?"

"That's a good idea," Corinne says and picks up her phone

We occupy the next hour by scouring local news and social media pages until all our phone batteries die.

"There aren't any reports of major accidents at the closure. That's promising," Amelia says. "And they have crews working on the downed power lines."

Someone's stomach growls so loudly we all hear it.

"Tanner is fine. I'm sure of it." There are so many things I want to say to him, do with him. I'm not me without him.

In the kitchen, I rummage through the pantry and fridge for anything that we can eat without the microwave or oven. "Does anyone else want a peanut butter and jelly sandwich?" I offer as I start to make myself one.

"I'm not that desperate yet," Tara says dismissively, but Amelia comes to the kitchen and I hand her the supplies.

"Thanks." Her voice is no more than a whisper.

For as friendly as Tara acted toward Amelia, they're not too chummy now which makes me wonder what happened after I left. I'll burn in hell before asking.

As it gets darker outside, the mood shifts inside. Tara gets less snarky and the genuine concern for her brother is more apparent. She shuts down, sitting on the couch with her legs pulled up and staring out into the night.

I grab the candles from the spare bedroom, so we have

more light in the living room and then I go to the game closet for a deck of cards and settle on the floor. As I lay out the cards for Solitaire, Tara makes an annoyed sound deep in her throat. "How are you sitting around playing cards right now? Do you even care if Tanner is okay? Or maybe you'll just move on to the next guy and ruin his life too. One hot jock is as good as the next."

"How dare you." The cards bend as I fist my hands with anger. "You don't get to judge me. You know absolutely nothing about me. Of course, I care if he's okay. The thought of something happening to him." I shake my head as my stomach clenches. "I can't even fathom it."

"We should be out there looking for him." She stands and motions with a big wave of her hand toward the window.

"He said to stay put." Though, I agree it feels awful not doing anything. "Besides, the road is closed. How far can we get?"

"Farther than we can sitting here." She resumes her position on the couch, hugging her knees.

"Well, let's go then. We'll go as far as we can."

"You're serious?" she asks.

"You're right, it beats sitting here. The rain has slowed so the roads should be safer." She doesn't move. Maybe she still thinks I'm kidding. "It's what Tanner would do if it were any of us."

And if it shuts her up, all the better.

Chapter Twenty-Five

SYDNEY

The four of us pile into Tara's small car. None of us had thought of charging our phones in the car before, but eagerly take turns plugging our phones in and turning them on to check for messages.

The road in the Shaw's lake house subdivision is quiet and the few vehicles we encounter are going as slow as we are. The rain is just a drizzle, but there's an eerie feeling being out when the houses all along are dark from the power outage.

We go on as far as we can until a police barricade prevents us from getting any closer to the highway. Tara pulls over on the side of the road and puts on her flashers. "I'm going to walk from here."

"Walk? And do what?" Corinne asks from the back seat. "They're not going to let you through on foot."

We've learned absolutely nothing and there's no sign of Tanner or his Firebird. I'm going to duct tape a charger into his car so he can never take it out again.

"We can at least ask them if they have any update on the road reopening or cars stranded on the other side." I glance around the car. Amelia and Corinne don't look like they love this idea. "You two stay here. Tara and I'll go."

Tara's brow quirks slightly in surprise, but she doesn't protest. The wind whips around us as we walk in silence along the side of the road.

"Tanner is probably sitting somewhere in a warm restaurant chowing down and watching TV. He'd have a good laugh at the two of us." I try to lighten the mood.

"Or at the bar." She snorts and pulls her jacket tighter around her stomach.

"No, not the bar. He doesn't drink if he knows he has to drive, and he'll be wanting to get home as soon as he can."

She regards me seriously and gives me a slight nod. When we get within earshot of the barricade, one of the police officers notices us and walks toward us.

"The road is closed ahead. We're not letting anyone through—cars or pedestrians."

"We don't want to get through. We just want to know how much longer it'll be?" Tara asks.

"We have someone stuck on the other side who can't get home," I add.

He rests his hands on his belt. "It's going to be a while still. We've got a crew cleaning up from the wreck and there's the tree and the power lines... anyone needing through is going to be waiting a bit, I'm afraid."

Tara's lower lip trembles.

It's the first anyone's mentioned an accident at the closing.

"Can you tell us who was in the accident or the model of the vehicle?"

"Smaller vehicle, a Fusion, I think. Everyone was stable and alert when the ambulance left for the hospital."

"Thank you," I manage for the both of us.

With a nod, he dismisses us, and Tara and I head back.

"Maybe by now he's realized he's not getting through any time soon and he's headed to Jonah's. I'm sure he'll call when—"

"This is all your fault." She stomps her foot and makes fists with her hands at her side. "If you hadn't left, he wouldn't have chased after you and he wouldn't be stranded in the middle of nowhere or on his way to the hospital while I'm stuck with you."

My mouth falls open. Every time I think she can't hurt me any worse, she somehow manages. "I left because of you. What is your problem?"

"Girls like you are my problem. I know your type. You hang around the jock houses, you're friendly with all the guys, and you're a convenient fuck that screws up their lives and wrecks any real relationships that comes along. You're beautiful and *fun*," she says the word like it's the worst trait possible. "And no sane girl wants to try to compete with that."

My face heats, and a chill runs up my spine. I've never been so angry in my entire life. "I am not a convenient fuck. Tanner and I were friends, nothing more until this summer. But you're right, *I've* been there. Through every relationship, I was there to tell him when he was being an ass. When he needed a shoulder to lean on or someone to talk it out... I. WAS. THERE." I grind my teeth down on every word. "I've been there through it all, not because I was hoping to trick him into sleeping with me but because I care about him. I want him to be happy. It's all I've ever wanted. So, don't you dare lump me into some stereotype jersey chaser."

She starts to cry, which is definitely not the reaction I expected. My anger dissipates into confusion and then guilt for being angry at someone who is clearly having a meltdown. I'm still pissed, for sure, but it's hard to feel good about kicking someone when they're down.

I have no idea what to do. How do you comfort someone who hates you? I watch her shoulders shake as silent tears slide down her cheeks. Tentatively, I reach out and touch her arm. "He's going to be okay, I promise."

It's a promise I have no business making, but I know what he means to her. She may hate me, but she loves her brother deeply and she's scared.

She throws her arms around me and sobs into my shirt. Stunned, I pat her back gingerly and let her squeeze me like a human teddy bear. For several moments, she cries while I hold still letting her use me for whatever consoling she needs. I'm half afraid this is her attempt to strangle me, but her arms stay at my waist.

When her tears slow, she sniffs and says, "I still don't like you."

A shocked laugh rips through me before I can stop it. "Yeah, I don't like you very much either."

We amble back to the car without saying another word.

"Well?" Corinne asks.

Tara stiffens her shoulders and pulls out onto the road. "He's fine. He's going to be fine," she says without any conviction in her tone.

She drives back to the house without any snarky remarks or evil glares in my direction. Her somber mood doesn't make me feel any better. When we get back, I'm the last to go inside. I linger on the front porch, looking out into the night. Where the hell are you, Tanner?

I swallow the lump in my throat and go in the house.

"I'm beat," Amelia says. "Is it okay if I crash here tonight? It doesn't look like I'm going to be able to leave until morning when the road is open. Tanner said I could stay, but I don't think he meant all night."

Tara shrugs from her reclaimed spot on the couch.

"You can stay in the spare room," I tell her. "Come on, I'll show you."

We take a couple of the candles with us, so she has light.

"Thank you." Amelia sits at the head of the bed and hugs a pillow to her chest. "I'm sorry about all this."

"Can I ask you something?"

"Of course."

I take a seat on the end of the bed and face her. "Was it my fault?" Tara certainly thinks it is, but she wasn't there. "I've been going over it and over it all day. Replaying times that the three of us were together and the things I might have said or done..."

"No." Her voice has a slight lift to it, and she laughs. "You were always so adamant that you were just friends. I thought you must be holding on to him any way you could and hoping he'd return the feelings someday. Believing that kept me from facing the fact that what he and I had felt inferior to what he had with you. He's different with you. He always has been." I can make out her small smile in in the mostly dark room. "It wasn't your fault any more than it was Tanner's. You two just fit together. I want that."

"Thank you. He cares about you a lot. I know that probably doesn't help, but I thought you should know."

I stand and start out of the room, but Amelia stops me. "Sydney?"

"Yeah."

"Tara will come around. She loves Tanner too much to stand in the way of anything that makes him happy, and you make him happier than anything. She'll realize that."

I want to believe that's true. I really do.

Corinne must have gone to bed, too, because it's just Tara in the living room when I leave Amelia.

I grab two beers and offer her one. "Here. A peace offering. I don't want to fight with you."

"Warm beer is your idea of a peace offering?" She makes no move to take it. "Besides, I don't want a peace offering. I don't think you're right for my brother. You're not going to convince me of that with any amount of alcohol."

I set it on the coffee table with a thud. "You know what, take it or don't, but stop pretending that this is about looking out for Tanner. This is your issue. Whatever story you've made up to make yourself feel better about treating me like shit, that's on you. I don't need to convince you of anything, but I hoped that you and I could find a way to get along for his sake. God, I actually thought we might be friends. How dumb was I? But, regardless, I'm not going anywhere, no matter what awful things you say or do to try to get rid of me. You're only hurting your brother."

With my beer, I sit on the floor and grab the cards I abandoned earlier. I'm finishing up my second game of Solitaire when she finally pops the top of the beer and we settle in to wait for Tanner.

It isn't exactly peaceful, but we've both said our peace anyway.

Chapter Twenty-Six

TANNER

I can barely keep my eyes open as I walk up to the front of the house. It's after three in the morning and the little sleep I got in my truck wasn't restful at all. Stuck in traffic for two hours and then by the time I could go anywhere, the only way they were letting anyone go was in the other direction.

Most people, saner than me, turned around, got a hotel, or went somewhere to wait it out. I pulled off into a parking lot as close to the highway as I could find and stayed. With no cell phone, there wasn't a lot to do except stare out into the night and think.

So, that's what I did. I thought about whether or not I'm going to play baseball or basketball next year. Both? I thought about my future and what I wanted after college. I thought about this summer and how great it's been. And I thought about Sydney. Mostly about Sydney.

How does she fit into all of it? What dreams does she have for the future and for us? We haven't talked about it, but I want to. I want to give her whatever she wants. Big dreams, epic life. Everything she deserves.

The house is quiet, and I shut the door behind me softly. The lights are out, but the microwave clock flashes and there are candles lit around the whole front living area. I'd heard the electricity was off in the area, but it looks like they managed. Eucalyptus and pear have never smelled so good.

Two forms are lying in the living room. As I get closer, I identify the one on the couch as Tara and the other is Sydney on the floor. Her eyes are closed, but even in sleep, her phone is in her hand as if she's been waiting for me to call.

I've been thinking about what it'd feel like to be back here, hugging her, all night. I swear those hours felt like weeks. I'm not sure why she left in the first place. Maybe she really thought there was a chance I'd get back with Amelia or maybe she's pissed at Tara—that'd make two of us. But whatever the reason, I don't want her to run when she's upset. I want to be her person even when she needs someone to vent to or punch. Though, she's punched me before and it fucking hurt, so I hope that's not what she needs right now. I'm so tired it might knock me on my ass.

I'm still staring at her, blonde hair splayed out, the comforter from the bed tossed over her, feet sticking out, when her eyes flutter open. She lifts her head slowly. "Tanner?"

She scrambles to her feet, but I can't make mine move. I manage to open my arms and brace myself before she throws herself around me.

"You're really here, right? I'm not dreaming?"

I run a hand down the back of her head, tangling my fingers through her hair. "I'm really here."

"Are you okay? What happened? Never mind, just kiss me."

"What if I'm not okay?" I chuckle as I bring my lips to hers.

"Then you better make it a good one that I can remember you by."

Sweeping my tongue into her mouth and digging my fingers against her back, I try to somehow get her closer. I don't worry about it being one to remember me by because I'm not going anywhere.

Funny how something as simple as being cut off from the ones you love for half a day can put things in perspective.

"Tanner?" Tara's groggy voice pulls at my attention.

Sydney and I break apart and I set her down. She moves to my side as Tara hurries to me.

"Oh my god, I was so scared." She's crying as she buries her face into my chest, then pulls back and smacks me on the arm.

"Ow! What was that for?"

"For scaring the crap out of us."

"I'm sorry. My phone died and I didn't have my charger." Another slap. "The highway was closed. They wouldn't let anyone through."

She nods and sniffs. "I know. We went out looking for you and saw the barricade. We called everyone we knew trying to find you." Her eyes widen. "You have to call Mom and Dad."

I wince thinking of my mom freaking out. "Do me a favor? Call them for me. My phone needs to charge, and I need to catch up with my girl. Please?"

She hesitates, glances between me and Sydney, but then agrees. "You owe me, though. For this and for taking a good five years off my life last night with all the worrying."

"I'll make it up to you later. Boat ride in the morning? We'll go to that place with the biscuits and gravy." I'm still pissed at the shenanigans she pulled today or yesterday, whatever day that was, but now is not the time to hash it out.

"Buying my love with food? Nice."

"You know it." I wink at her and add, "Love you, sis."

With a burst of adrenaline fueled from exhaustion and the prospect of kissing her until I pass out, I grab Sydney's legs and toss her over my shoulder.

"Wait," Tara calls after us. "It's already morning. What time?"

"*Tomorrow* morning," I clarify and shut the door before she can yell at me some more. For the next twenty-four hours I'm not leaving this room. I need to sleep for half of it and make out with Sydney for the other half.

"She was really worried about you." Sydney pulls me down on top of her as soon as I lay her on the bed.

"Not you?"

"I knew you were okay. You had to be. I refused to believe that I'd just gotten you and then lost you." Her brown eyes soften, and she swallows. "I shouldn't have left. I've waited so long for this and then I ran at the first bump in the road because I was afraid that after all this time, I'd somehow lucked into it out of lack of options."

My lips twitch at the ridiculous notion, but she doesn't give me time to correct her before she continues. "But, I don't care. Even if the only reason you want to be with me now is because I ruined things with Amelia and every other girl you dated and I'm the last woman on the island, so to speak, I'm still the best option because no one loves you more than me. Not now, not ever. I came back to tell you that I'm going to fight for you."

"Hot as that sounds, it's no contest. You win by a knockout every time. It's me and you babe." I rest my forehead against hers. "I'm so ridiculously in love with my best friend."

As I bring my lips to hers gently, I feel hers pull up into a smile. "Say it again."

"I am in love with you, Sydney Turner. Stupid in love and,

not to cheapen the moment, but I'd very much like to get you naked now."

Her sweet laughter fills the room and then she pulls her T-shirt over her head and unsnaps the bright pink lacy bra and discards it as well.

"Better?" she asks with a cheeky tone.

I bring my hands up to her chest and cup her breasts. Her skin is so warm and soft. "So much."

She tugs at the hem of my T-shirt and I reach around with one arm and pull it over my head. With a sigh, she glides both palms over my abs and chest. "Someday I want to test the theory of washboard abs."

"You want to do laundry on my stomach?"

She grins and looks up to the ceiling, eyes scrunched as if she's considering her answer. "Maybe not laundry, but something sudsy with water and sponges.... Ooooh, maybe you could wash my car."

"Or we should take a bath."

"I like my idea better."

The grin and her cheeky banter stop when I lean forward and kiss the valley between her breasts. I trail my mouth along every bare inch of skin. Goose bumps rise to the surface and I double back to kiss those too.

She's wearing a pair of tight black leggings that are hard to wiggle off, so I give up and push her legs apart and bring my mouth to her center. Over the material, I nip and suck. Sydney shoves the leggings down for me, eager for more, and when she's bare, I repeat it all with no barrier.

Her hands find my shoulders and then comb through my hair. She makes the hottest noises of encouragement and writhes beneath me.

Toned and athletic, long and lean. I've heard her grumbling

about her small boobs or lack of curves, but Sydney's body is phenomenal. All those hours playing volleyball and working out to be better at her sport have sculpted her body into this beautiful and powerful thing.

As her moans get louder signaling she's close, I pull back and stare down at her spread open to me.

"Turn over, baby. On your hands and knees."

She complies quickly with no hesitation. I love how eager she is and how easily she lets me take control. I'd give her anything she wanted, and I think she knows that, but there's something hot about being allowed temporary power over this amazing woman.

I swat her butt playfully and then place a kiss on her spine. Wrapping a hand around my dick, I give myself a quick jerk before lining up at her entrance.

Sydney glances over her shoulder and we lock eyes as I push inside of her. I don't know if anything has ever felt better. Not hitting a game winning shot and not striking out a batter in the bottom of the ninth. For a guy who's constantly chasing the high of winning, sex has sometimes felt like a letdown. Not that I didn't enjoy it, because duh even bad sex is awesome, but nothing has ever come close to those adrenaline-fueled, bigger than life moments sports have given me.

Sydney does. She's all the best parts of a teammate, a coach, and an opponent wrapped up in one sexy as hell package. But the best part about spending time with Sydney is that I see myself outside of the identities I've clung to. I'm stripped down to my core with her. I'm not a basketball player or a baseball player, I'm just a guy enjoying the moment.

With one hand on her back and the other at her hip, I pump into her at a hard and steady rhythm. Sydney's head falls to the mattress and her back arches. My name slips from her mouth with a groan as the orgasm shatters her beneath me.

Her pussy squeezes me and tips me over the edge. Even after we've both come, she moves her hips in a small circle, milking me for every drop.

We both groan as I withdraw. She slumps onto the bed to her back. A sheen of sweat covers her body and glistens in the dark of the room.

I cover her body with mine and my dick twitches between us. Her lips pull up into a smile. "Tell the big guy, I said hey, but I need a minute."

"Yeah?" I rub myself against her pussy. "Well, while you take a minute, he wants to say hey back."

Her eyelids fall shut. "I like the way he says hello better than when you do."

I chuckle. "I'll remember that, babe."

"It looks like a bomb went off in here," I say as I survey the bedroom. Sheets and pillows are scattered around. I think we fucked in every square inch of this room. "I'm going to take Tara out for breakfast, and then when I come back, let's take the boat out. I owe you a driving lesson." There isn't any of the excitement I expected on her face. "Do you not want to learn?"

"It isn't that."

I sit back on the edge of the bed. Sydney wears her emotions all over her face, but I can't figure out what this one is—nerves? Fear?

"Your sister hates me. We... *I* said some things I shouldn't have. I'm sorry. I hate the position that puts you in."

"I'm sure she deserved whatever you said. I don't know what her problem is, but I'm not worried."

"You're not? Why? Your family is so important to you."

"They are. So are you. Besides, I know you. You'll win her over no matter how hard she tries to dislike you."

"I think you overestimate my charm." She smiles, but then it falls. "That's what I don't get, though. Why does she want to dislike me?"

"I'm not sure, but let me worry about Tara." I stand and pull on my T-shirt. "You'll text me after your appointment and let me know how it goes?"

"Yeah. Fingers crossed for good news."

"Fingers crossed." I lean forward and take her lips. An entire day in this bed and it's still hard to pull myself away. "We'll celebrate later."

"You're going to yell at me now, aren't you?" Tara asks when we're seated at the restaurant. "Busy place where I can't make a scene and I'm stranded with a lake between me and my car."

"When have I ever yelled at you?" I roll my eyes. "I do want to know what the hell is going on with you though. You haven't been yourself—and I don't just mean the shit with Sydney. You seem different. I mean, you haven't even commented on the fact I'm wearing a boring white T-shirt today."

"I gave up on changing your fashion sense years ago." She plays with the sugar holder on the table. "I met a guy."

A groan escapes my lips before I can stop it. "A guy?"

"Do you want to know or not?"

"Yeah." I run a hand through my hair. "Yeah, I do." I hope

I don't have to hunt some dude down after breakfast and kick his ass.

"He's great. We have tons in common and we get along really well. I've known him since freshman year, same friends and all that. We hung out a few times just the two of us and I thought he really liked me, but then..." She hesitates.

"You slept with him?"

She nods. "And that was it. He moved on to the next girl, some chick that's always hanging around the soccer house sleeping with all the guys."

"I'm sorry, Tara. I really am. The guy sounds like an asshole and not worth it."

"Maybe, or maybe I made it too easy on him. I should have made him wait longer or, I don't know, something. He moved right along to the next easy girl who came along."

"Listen, if things with Sydney have taught me anything, it's that when the right person comes along you have to take a chance, no holding back. You did that and it bit you in the ass, but it won't always."

"Or maybe you two are together because it's easy. She's always around, and—"

"Stop. I appreciate your concern, but it really isn't any of your business. She isn't an article of clothing I'm asking your opinion on. I love her, she's my best friend, and I want to be with her for... a long time, maybe forever."

Tara's eyes widen. "Forever? You're not going to do something stupid and get engaged before you've even graduated college, are you? I wanted you to have a life, but let's pump the breaks."

I chuckle. "I think I'll give dating a whirl for a while first, but she's not going anywhere. And I think you two have a lot more in common than you think."

My sister looks skeptical.

"That story you just told me? Sydney has one pretty similar to it. It's not mine to tell, but she's been hurt before, too. She knows what it's like. Listen, I'm not asking that you become friends with her. I know you liked Amelia, I did too, but she wasn't right for me. I need you to understand that hurting Sydney is only going to put a wedge between us. I know you don't want that and neither do I. And you owe her an apology. Inviting Amelia down, no matter how much you like her, was super uncool."

"I know." She sighs and lets out a breath. "Are we good?"

"Apologize to Sydney, and then, yeah, we're good."

She sits back in her chair and I mimic her relaxed posture as I add cream and sugar to my coffee. "So, this guy, does he have a name? Address?"

"You're not going to hunt him down."

"No, but I might glitter bomb him."

A heavy body rolls on top of me and I groan. "It's too early for sex."

And my lady parts are sore from two days of makeup sex. It feels like we've made up for way more than two years' worth of missed opportunities.

"Emily's here."

My eyes fly open and I struggle to move under Tanner's weight.

"I'm going to try not to be offended that you're suddenly wide awake and anxious to get out of this bed," he says as he moves off me.

I put on a pair of shorts and a T-shirt and brush my lips against his. "Will you take us out on the boat this morning?"

He grabs me around the waist and pulls me back down onto the bed. His hand slides under my shirt and cups me over the lacy material of my bra. Those lady parts I said were too sore? They don't care about my well-being at all as Tanner rubs his thumb back and forth over a nipple.

As quick as he started, he removes his hand and hops up. "I'll be ready in five."

"You're an evil man, Tanner Shaw." I right my shirt and take a steadying breath before I go find Emily.

My friend stands from a stool at the kitchen counter with a knowing smirk. "Hard to pull yourself out of bed these days now that there's a boy in it, huh?"

"You made it." I hug her middle and squeeze tight.

She steps back and eyes me closely. "You are so tan. You bitch."

"A few days here and you will be, too." I go to the fridge and grab two waters and then lead her out to the deck. "Tanner is going to take us out this morning and then there's some big Fourth of July party at his friend Jonah's house this afternoon."

"Is the evil sister coming with us?" she whispers.

"I doubt they're here. She and Corinne have started going over to the local gym to do yoga in the mornings, but she'll be at Jonah's party, yeah."

Things with Tara have been awkward, but she hasn't been outright mean since the night of the storm. I don't have any delusions that she has suddenly started to like me, but I'm worrying less about her coming between me and Tanner. I have to make peace with the idea that she may never like me.

I don't know what I would do if I had a sister who hated Tanner. Emily's the closest thing to it, but she and Tanner get along great.

"I can't wait to meet her."

"Please don't say anything. I said my peace; she said hers. It puts Tanner in an awful position and today is supposed to be fun. One last big celebration before our senior year."

"All right," she concedes. "But if she so much as looks at you the wrong way, I'm not going to be able to hold back."

"Fair enough."

Emily and Jonah hit it off right away. He wraps an arm around her shoulder and leads her into the middle of the party to introduce her to people.

"Come on, I have a surprise for you." Tanner takes my hand and we weave through the people in the back yard at Jonah's house.

Where the badminton net stood the last time I was here is a volleyball court—complete with sand.

"How?" I ask excitedly as I kick off my sandals and walk onto the hot sand. I close my eyes as it seeps between my toes.

"Every Fourth of July party needs an activity. I convinced Jonah this year's needed sand volleyball."

"Thank you. This is amazing."

"And it gives you a chance to try out that new shoulder."

"How long have you been planning this?" I ask as I walk around the perimeter. This took a lot of work to bring in all the sand alone.

"A while," he admits.

"What if my shoulder hadn't healed?"

"We'd have spent the day on the other side of the yard, and I would have hoped like hell you didn't notice."

He leans down and picks up the volleyball and tosses it to me. "What do you say?"

"I say I want you on my team this time."

We grab Emily and Jonah to play against us. We're pretty evenly matched with two volleyball players and two tall, athletic dudes, but Tanner's and my familiarity with each other and the way we can communicate without saying anything at all, means we work better together as a team.

"Not fair," Jonah says after the first game. "You two have some sort of secret love language going on. Let's switch it up, boys versus girls."

Emily and I share an amused look.

"You want to play against us?" she asks.

"We can handle it," Jonah insists.

Emily walks over to my side with a bounce to her step. Tanner moves to the other with a shake of his head. "It's a good thing Richard isn't here to see you get your ass kicked by a couple of girls."

As the day turns to night and the sun begins its descent, the party doubles in size. People who spent the day at party cove now trickle in, including Tara and Corinne. They hang near the pool and Emily and I stay close to the volleyball court. I think we're both more anxious than we realized to get back to school and volleyball.

"I have to go help Jonah and Ollie set up the fireworks." Tanner stands and brushes off his shorts.

"Have to?"

"Want to." He grins. "I get to light shit on fire and watch it blow up." He kisses my cheek. "See you in a bit."

"Should we get another drink?" Emily asks. She gets to her feet and helps me up with both hands.

As we're filling our cups with beer, Tara and Corinne approach. Emily sees her first. "Evil sister-in-law is headed this way."

"You have to stop calling her that," I say with a laugh.

"Mhmmm. Well, at least I have a full cup of beer in case I need to throw it in her face."

I shush her with an elbow in the ribs.

"Hey," Tara says as I hand her the tap.

"This is my friend Emily." I motion with my head to her and glance at Emily's hard expression. "Em, this is Tanner's sister, Tara, and her friend, Corinne."

They exchange stiff smiles and mumbled hellos.

"Sydney, can I talk to you for a minute?" Tara asks.

Emily stands tall beside me. She's only slightly taller than me, but she can look downright intimidating when she wants to. And she wants to. I love how she always has my back, but I've got this.

"Sure."

Tara takes a step, as do I, to follow her, but Emily grabs my wrist. "If you need me, give me a signal. A hair flip or something."

"I'll be fine."

Though the longer she's silent and the farther we move away from the party, the more unsure I feel about my safety.

"Are you going to push me into the lake?" I ask with a tight laugh. "Because I can swim."

She stops and faces me. "I need to apologize to you."

"Okay." I wait for more that doesn't come. "Was *that* the apology?"

"I'm sorry for everything. Tanner has mentioned you a lot over the years and I made some judgments based on my own experiences of girls who hang around the jocks at my school. I should have spent the last two weeks getting to know you, but instead I was hell-bent on hating you on principle. Even so, inviting Amelia here was not my finest moment."

"People have never understood me and Tanner. We didn't even understand it ourselves until this past month." I shrug. "I meant what I said the other night. I hoped that you and I would be friends, but I think being civil should suffice. I only want to make Tanner happy."

"I'm starting to believe you."

The first firework shoots up into the sky over the water. "I should get back. I want to find Emily and get a seat." I step backward and offer her a small smile. "Thank you for apologizing."

"Sydney?" Tara calls to my back.

"Yeah." I angle my body slightly.

"I hope someday we can still be friends."

I'm not ready for that, but maybe someday... "I hope so, too."

Emily hands me my cup as I get close. "I found us the perfect spot. Come on."

She climbs up the ladder of the pool slide and sits at the top. I squeeze in next to her. "Comfort aside, this is a great spot."

She squirms. "I think I underestimated our combined width."

I rest my head on her shoulder. "I'm really glad you're here."

Another spark shoots up into the air. Red and blue dots the sky and falls. One after another. The music blasting at the party has changed to a patriotic playlist. It's the perfect end to the best summer ever.

"Yo, babe!" Tanner yells.

I glance around before a splash of water shoots up from the pool. He's standing in water up to his chest grinning at me.

"Get your sexy ass in here. I've been looking all over for you."

"I thought you were doing the fireworks."

"What?" he yells over another loud pop.

"I thought..." I shift my hips side to side to unglue myself from the spot. "Screw it," I mutter. I hand my phone over to Emily. "I'm going in."

Hands over head, I squeal with happiness as I go down the slide fully clothed. Tanner catches me at the bottom, but the force sends us underwater.

Strong hands glide up my body and frame my face before he kisses me. If breathing weren't necessary, it'd be a pretty great way to spend the rest of the night.

When we resurface, I wrap my arms around his neck, and he keeps us afloat.

"Who's doing the fireworks?" I ask as another set of three goes off.

We lift our heads toward the sky to watch as the lights slowly disappear leaving a trace of smoke behind.

"Jonah and Ollie."

"But you were so excited to blow shit up."

"Jonah let me have the first two. That was enough to get the fire bug out of my system for another year and now I get to watch the finale with you."

We adjust so that my back is against his front. He wraps his arms around me, and I lean my head against his chest.

"Best summer ever," he whispers next to my ear. "How are we going to top it next year?"

"I'm not sure, but I'm looking forward to it."

As I walk onto the court at the fieldhouse, I breathe in the musty smell, the squeak of shoes, and the laughter and raised voices of the guys joking around.

A guy I recognize but haven't met is talking with Datson. They look up as I approach.

Datson spins a ball between his palms. "Shaw, have you met Cameron Reed?"

"No." I extend a hand to the sophomore transfer. "Nice to meet you."

"Same."

"Are you guys working on drills or just shooting around?" Official practices won't start for a while yet, but most of the guys are back at Valley already and we'll start conditioning and lifting together in the morning, and in the afternoons, we'll most likely all show up to shoot around or work on agility drills. It's a chance for us to find a rhythm again before school and regular workouts begin.

"Messing around," Datson says and does a once-over of my outfit. "Where have you been?"

I grab a ball from the rack. "I met with Coach Wiles."

"Oh yeah?" Datson pauses. "And?"

"And... I'm going to be busy again this year."

"Good for you, buddy."

"Yo, Shaw," Benny calls to me from the sideline where he chats with Lawson. "I heard you and Sydney finally hooked up."

Chuckling, I fire a shot at the basket. Benny rebounds and holds it, waiting for an answer. I glance over at Datson who smirks.

"They'd have found out eventually," he says by way of an excuse.

"We didn't *hook up*. We're together. She's my girlfriend."

"Congrats, man," Lawson says. He's one of the few guys on the team who has a steady girlfriend—the same one since our freshmen year.

"Thanks." It feels weird to finally call her my girlfriend. Amazing but weird.

We shoot hoops and get to know Cameron. He's a bit of a mystery, not because he's quiet or shy—he isn't, but because he transferred from one of the best college basketball programs in the country after only one year. He played as a freshman and even helped take his team to the final four. They were a young team, and everyone was already speculating that they'd make it back to the championship again this coming year.

Our Valley record is nothing to laugh at. We won the national championship my freshman year and the past two years we've done all right, but not so well that I can understand why he'd transfer.

We're lucky to have him, though, and he seems like a decent guy. We're finishing up when Wes, one of our assistant coaches, walks onto the court and juts his chin to me with a tilt of his head. "Shaw, can I talk to you?"

"Uh-oh," Datson whispers. Or his version of a whisper, but it's loud enough I'm sure Wes heard it.

I hand Datson the ball and walk off to meet Wes who hovers on the sideline.

"How was your summer?" he asks, though I can tell it isn't why he called me over. Wes is a great coach, but small talk is not his thing.

"Good. Yours?"

"Good. Yeah, really good." He shifts uncomfortably. "Listen, I heard you talked with Coach Wiles, and you're planning to keep playing baseball this year."

Shit, news travels fast. I thought I had at least through the weekend before everyone found out. It isn't that I wanted to hide it, hardly anyone even knew I was seriously considering quitting baseball, but I wanted to give it a little more time to adjust to the decision myself.

"Yeah, that's right. I know you hate that I'm doing both, but I promise when I'm here, I'm here."

"I don't hate it," he starts. "Well, okay, I totally hate it, but you've proven you can manage both. It can't have been easy to juggle everything. I admire your dedication to both."

I'm slack-jawed. This from the guy who spent my freshman year telling me I needed to choose one or the other. God, he was a pain in the ass. I looked up to him. He was a senior on the team then and I watched how he led the team on and off the court. I wanted to be him, and he wanted me to get lost.

"Thanks, I think," I say with a chuckle.

One side of his mouth pulls up into a grin and he takes a step away. "Don't think I'm going to start taking it easy on you or anything though."

"Bring it, Coach."

Sydney and Emily moved into an apartment off campus and she's been busy getting that set up all day, so by the time she stops by The White House it's dark and a small party has formed.

I get up from my chair when she walks outside and meet her halfway.

"Hey, how's the apartment looking?" I drop a kiss to her lips and lead her inside to get her something to drink.

"Good. It's coming together. Emily had to try the living room furniture in every possible arrangement before she'd make a decision on which she liked best."

"I can't wait to see it."

"Make sure to tell Em how well it flows." She lowers her voice as her roommate walks toward us.

"Hey guys," she says. Emily has this bounce to her step and a bubbly personality that makes her seem all sweet and inno-cent, but she can turn that sweet to sour on a dime when someone pisses her off.

"Hey, Em, congrats on the apartment and on your flow."

One brow lifts, and she slides her gaze to Sydney. "My flow?"

My girl laughs. "The flow of the... you know what, never mind."

I hand Sydney the Malibu and grab the Coke from the fridge.

"Is the new transfer guy here?" Emily asks, craning her neck to see outside. "I heard he's hot."

Sydney puts her hands up defensively. "She didn't hear it from me."

"He's in the pool," I say.

Emily starts toward the door and pauses. "Don't forget," she says to Sydney. "First night in the new place, you're coming home with me."

I wrap my arms around Sydney. "We'll see."

"You had her all summer, Shaw. It's time to share."

"I knew we should have stayed at the lake."

She turns around to face me and brings her arms to my chest. "How'd it go with Coach Wiles?"

"Good, I think. I'm going to continue to do both. Maybe it's the last year that I'll get to do that and maybe I'm risking my chance to get drafted to the NBA, but I'm willing to take the risk. Quitting either one just didn't feel right."

"I'm proud of you."

"Wes told me he admired me." I shake my head. "He's the last person I expected to hear that from. Coach was happy because he knew if I was going to quit one it was probably baseball, but I assumed everyone else was hoping I'd pick one or the other."

"You can handle both. You're the most hardworking and dedicated person I know. I have no doubt that you'll crush it this year and get drafted to the NBA *and* MLB next year and I'm excited to travel all around and cheer you on at both."

"You would do that? Travel to games and events and stuff?"

"If you wanted me to, yeah." She stares at me with a weird expression. "You seem surprised? Am I freaking you out? Is it too soon to say things like that?" She cringes. "Sorry, it feels like we've been together a lot longer than we have."

"I'm not freaked out," I assure her. "I'm surprised, but in a good way. That's a lot to ask of someone. I have no idea where I'll end up and it might change year to year."

She shrugs. "I want to be where you are."

"Even tonight?"

"Nice try. I promised Emily."

"Well, fine, I'm stealing you now, then. Grab your drink."

I lead her up the stairs and to my room. Hesitating at the door, I squeeze her hand. "Remember that night you came over to the house with Nathan and Chloe, after we'd all gone to The Hideout?"

"Of course. That was the night we first kissed and then I opened my big mouth and told you I wasn't going to sleep with you. How dumb was I?"

I chuckle. "It worked out okay."

"Yeah, but all those years of missed sex."

"Well, I might have a solution of sorts for that." I open the door and let her go in first.

"Tanner, oh my gosh." She walks in, stops, and glances back at me with wide eyes and mouth open. "What is this?"

"It's date number five."

"It's perfect."

I finally move into the room with her and shut the door. Not half bad, I have to admit. I bought a bunch of twinkle lights and strung them around the room, much safer than candles since I wasn't sure how long before I could get her up here and they don't smell like weird combinations of food and flowers. Speaking of, I also bought flowers and placed them in vases around the room. Colorful bouquets in yellows, oranges, and bright pinks. Roses didn't feel right. Too predictable and too boring.

She walks to me and rests her hands on my shoulder. "You didn't need to do all this to make up for the past."

"I didn't."

She looks unconvinced.

"I admit that before this summer I always felt like I missed my shot and when we finally got together I wanted to do everything I could to make up for it, but the thing is you've always been exactly what I needed, when I needed it, and I wouldn't change that. But now, I need you to be my girl." I graze my teeth lightly along her neck. "Today, tomorrow, ten years from now... it's always going to be me and you. I love you. So, this, date number five isn't about looking back—it's about celebrating it all."

"I like the sound of that." She tilts her head to give me better access and then pulls back with a sigh. "Emily's going to kill me."

"We'll stay at your place tomorrow night," I promise.

Sydney pulls away and flops onto my bed. She taps a button on her phone and music starts playing. "Okay, let's see your moves?"

"My moves?"

"Oh, I'm sorry. Did you have a special song picked out?"

"A special song? What the hell are you talking about?"

Her mouth puckers into a smug smile. "I believe I was promised a striptease on date number five. Don't think I forgot."

I toss my head back and laugh. "Anything you want, babe."

EPILOGUE
Sydney

Two years later

"I think I might puke... or shit myself," Tanner says, voice high and tight.

"Charming. I'll be the laughingstock of the Wags section. They'll call you Skidmark and I'll be Skidmark's girl."

"Skidmark's fiancée," he corrects me, suddenly sounding calmer.

"You're going to be great. I'm going to FaceTime Tara and the new boyfriend so we can watch the game together."

He grunts.

Over the past two years, Tara has dated a series of guys, each one worse than the last. I admire her perseverance, but I really hope this one works out so Tanner can stop adding guys to his glitter bomb hit list. She and I have slowly become friendly. We don't have girls' nights out or gab on the phone, but we both always show up to support Tanner and I think we've found a mutual respect for one another.

"All right. I've got to go. We're pulling up to the arena. I'll call you after the game. Will you still be up?" he asks.

"You think I'm going to bed early on my superstar fiancé's first night playing in an NBA game?"

"Well you're like four hours ahead."

"Three. You're really going to have to figure out the time zones."

"If the other states would stop doing daylight's savings time like Arizona did, it would be so much easier. Half the year it's two hours. The other half it's three. Who can store all that useless information?"

"You're rambling," I say, biting back a smile. It's rare that I've seen, or heard, Tanner this spun up. Not that I can blame him. He's worked hard for this. The past year since we graduated from Valley hasn't been easy. He signed with the Celtics and the Red Sox. The media went nuts and my boyfriend—now fiancé—became a sensation. His handsome face was everywhere I went for a while—magazines, TV, social media. It was super trippy.

So was moving to Boston. In what universe did I end up living somewhere so cold? At least I have the beach.

Then, he got hurt. He was nervous that it was all going to blow up, but he worked twice as hard and tonight he finally gets to play in their game against the Lakers in Los Angeles.

"I'm fucking nervous."

"You are going to be amazing," I say for what is probably the hundredth time this week. "I can't wait to watch. I'm going to call Tara; do you want to stay on the line and say hi?"

"Nah, we're getting off the bus. Tell her I said hi and apologize in advance that she's about to be known as Skidmark's sister."

"You're so dramatic. I am not telling her that. Good luck. I love you. Don't shit your pants."

He chuckles. "Love you, too. Bye, babe."

I drop my phone into my clutch as I approach Tara.

"Was that Tanner?" she asks as we share a quick hug hello.

"Yeah, he says hi."

She glances around. "Does he know we're here?"

"He has no clue. He thinks I am FaceTiming with you and Steve for the game."

She makes a face. "That's over."

"I liked Steve."

"His penis was like..." She holds up her hand to show me just how small and I wave her off.

"Got it. Okay. Well, Tanner's teammate, Henry, left tickets for us at will call so we can sit behind the bench with the Wags."

Tara takes a bunch of pictures of us outside the arena that we can tease Tanner with later. Then we fall into line with the other fans and navigate to our seats.

"Oh, man, I feel like I might be sick. I'm so nervous for him." Tara holds a hand to her stomach.

I seem to be the only one of us who isn't worried. He's got this. I've never had any doubts that Tanner would be here one day or that I'd be on the sidelines cheering him on. There was a time I wouldn't have believed I'd be doing it as his fiancée, but I've always believed in him.

"There he is!" Tara squeezes my arm and stops in the middle of the aisle. The guys are on the floor in their green uniforms. He looks calmer now as he palms a basketball and scans the arena. He's taking it all in and I'm so glad to be here to witness this. Nothing he could do in the game would be as good as seeing him finally walk out with his team knowing he's going to do something besides sit on the sideline.

Tara screams his name and waves her hands over her head. She has absolutely no chill. He looks down, avoiding eye contact with the crazed fan yelling his name, but Henry nudges him and points toward us.

Tara keeps waving until he spots us. His mouth slowly pulls into a huge grin and he moves toward us.

We go down as far as we can. It's still early, so many of the seats are empty.

"Surprise!" Tara says as he gets to us.

He shakes his head. "What are you two doing here?"

"You didn't really think we'd miss this?" She rolls her eyes at her brother and then pulls back, leaving me room to step up to him.

"You're here." He squeezes me hard against him and I swear I can feel some of his nerves fall away. He smells like laundry detergent and leather and something that's just Tanner. He left yesterday morning to fly up with the team, but it feels like so much longer. I've never once regretted my decision to move with him to Boston. I get how that might be a big deal to some people, but there's nothing I love more than being with him. Arizona, Massachusetts... I'd follow him to the ends of the earth.

Tanner

After the game, Sydney and Tara meet us at the hotel. We fly to Utah tomorrow for another game before we head back to Boston on Thursday. The road trips aren't as bad as I thought.

Although, admittedly much better when Sydney surprises me and shows up.

I open the door wide to let her and Tara into the hotel room I'm sharing with Henry.

He's kicked back on the couch with a beer. Another one of our teammates and buddies, Chris, is on his phone ordering enough room service to feed the entire hotel.

"I can't believe this is your life." Tara throws her arms around me again, hugging me in a vise grip and making it hard to breathe.

"Missed me?"

"Yes, so much."

"Missed you too, T." I ruffle her bangs—that's a new style since I've seen her last. "Let me introduce you to a couple of my teammates."

Sydney steps up beside me and I pull her against my hip.

"Guys," I say to get their attention. "This is my little sister, Tara."

"Oh my god, Tanner, you make it sound like I'm twelve." Tara swats at my chest and then takes a seat between them on the couch. "I'm in grad school."

"Cool," Henry says. "What school?"

I turn to Sydney. "Is it me or does she seem a little too cozy with my teammates for someone with a boyfriend?"

"Oh, uh..."

"No? They broke up already?"

"Apparently he has a small penis." My girl shrugs.

Ugh. "Oh man, I could have really gone without that information."

"If I had to know, so do you." She leans over and kisses me, successfully distracting me from thinking about my sister's ex-boyfriend's small dick. "Congratulations on the game. Ten points, two assists, pretty impressive."

"So sexy when you track my stats."

"To be honest, I double-checked after the game."

"Thank you for coming."

"You're welcome. I'm really glad I got to see it in person. The camera people have this awful habit of tracking the ball instead of you."

"I'll be easier to follow now that I'll be on the court instead of the bench." I lace my fingers behind her lower back and drop a kiss to her shoulder. "Seriously, thank you for being here. It was perfect. Work was cool about you taking the time off?"

"Oh yeah, they were fine. I've put in so many hours over the past month, they owed me. And the girls will be fine. They need grumpy Coach Bill occasionally, so they know how awesome I am."

"I'm sure they already know."

Sydney found a job with a local foundation in Boston coaching a youth girls beach volleyball team. She's amazing. The girls love her. Even the ones who it's clear were forced into it by parents or guardians end up having a blast.

"I do have to go back to Boston tomorrow though, so I'm sorry I can't follow the team to Utah."

"Then we'll make the most of tonight."

"Yeah? And how would you like to celebrate your professional basketball debut? Do you want to hang out here with the guys? We could all go out?"

"Sleeping?"

She chuckles.

"I'm so tired. Think Tara will notice if we disappear for a quick nap?"

"It's six o'clock. The sun hasn't even gone down. And we can't leave Tara. She wants to spend time with you."

I glance over to where she's talking with Henry. Turned to him, a hand resting on his arm. Yeah, I don't think she'll miss me.

"Real quick power nap. Sex for like twenty and then forty minutes to sleep. We'll be back in an hour."

"Sex for twenty?"

I run a hand through my hair. "Yeah, I was overselling it. I'm good for like maybe five minutes of sex, but, bonus, longer to nap."

She presses her body against mine and kisses me. She makes a little humming sound as she steps away and pulls me with her. "We should hang out. I promise that I'll still be good for quickie sex later."

I sit in a big armchair and tug Sydney down on my lap. Someone hands us both a beer. Tara's amped up and carries the conversation.

Me, I get to sit back, wrap my arms around my girl, and soak up the moment. I played in an NBA game today. I get paid to play basketball. And baseball. But the best part is I've got my best friend by my side.

PLAYLIST

- Head & Heart by Joel Corry feat. MNEK
- Right Back by Khalid feat. A Boogie Wit Da Hoodie
- Civil War by Russ
- Summer Feelings by Lennon Stella feat. Charlie Puth
- The Fix by Nelly feat. Jeremih
- Mood by 24kGoldn feat. Iann Dior
- So What! by jxdn
- Pretty Thang by Fetty Wap
- My Ex's Best Friend by Machine Gun Kelly feat. Blackbear
- Getting Started by Aloe Blacc feat. JID
- Come & Go by Juice WRLD feat. Marshmello
- Concert for Aliens by Machine Gun Kelly
- Lost in the Fire by Gesaffelstein and The Weeknd
- What You Know Bout Love by Pop Smoke
- Laugh Now Cry Later by Drake feat. Lil Durk

- All Girls Are The Same by Juice WRLD
- Lemonade by Internet Money feat. Gunna, Don Toliver, NAV
- Wonder by Shawn Mendes

ALSO BY REBECCA JENSHAK

Campus Nights Series

Secret Puck

Bad Crush

Smart Jocks Series

The Catch

The Assist

The Fadeaway

The Tip-Off

The Fake

The Pass

Standalone Novels

Sweet Spot

Electric Blue Love

Jilted Jock

SECRET PUCK SAMPLE

Continue reading for a preview of Secret Puck!

Secretly hooking up with the team captain's sister was a bad idea.

In my defense, the first time I saw her I didn't know who she was.

Kind, gorgeous, a little naïve. Ginny brightened my world from day one.

I knew I was no good for her. She was just out of a relationship and I had a reputation for having a new girl in my bed every weekend.

I tried to do the right thing. Honest.

I'm the one who insisted we should be just friends.

That lasted about as long as you'd expect.

But Ginny? She's the best—best friend, best everything.

So yeah, hooking up with the team captain's sister wasn't a great idea.

Would I do it again?

In a heartbeat.

CHAPTER 1

Ginny

"What are you doing here?" I ask my brother through a small crack in the door.

He leans his large frame against it, widening the gap and keeping me from closing it on him. "I'm checking on my favorite sister."

"I'm your only sister."

He pushes a big shoulder against it, and I give up on trying to keep him out. Crossing the small dorm room in three steps, I resume my position on the bed.

"Have you left the dorm at all this weekend?" He follows me and takes a seat at the end of my bed. "Hey, Ava."

My roommate Ava's on the phone with her boyfriend Trent, but waves and blushes when Adam acknowledges her.

"I'm enjoying my last days of summer vacation," I tell him as I pull my hair down from the messy bun and attempt to make it look like I haven't been rocking this same hairstyle for three days. It's the day before classes start and the only things going on around campus are parties and new student activities

—neither of which have sounded appealing enough to get dressed and leave my room.

He picks up the package of cheese and peanut butter crackers I'd been devouring when he knocked. "This looks like the opposite of fun. And you bailed on my party last night."

"A party with a bunch of your teammates... yeah, no thanks."

"You can't sit in here moping forever. Bryan did you a favor. Long-distance relationships in college suck. Next to no one survives them. Plus, the guy was a tool anyway. Don't let it ruin college. College is awesome."

My heart cracks a little more at the reminder that my ex-boyfriend, who should be with me at Valley starting our freshman year together, decided at the last minute to go to Idaho instead.

It wasn't entirely his fault. He got the offer after they'd lost their second-string quarterback to an injury. Bryan became their new second-string and I was cut from his roster altogether.

Adam nudges my arm with his elbow. "Come on. Let's grab lunch, or come over and hang at the apartment, meet my roommates. *You don't need no man. There's plenty of fish in the sea.* What kind of pep talk are you feeling?"

I smile. "Of course you think there's plenty of fish in the sea. You have a new girlfriend every semester."

"Exactly. I speak from experience."

I don't think it'll be that easy for me. My brother is a hockey player, tall and muscular, and I guess objectively he's attractive. He certainly has no problem finding girlfriends if that's any indication. He has perfect hair; I'll give him that. I've had hair envy my whole life. Where my dirty blonde hair is stuck somewhere between straight and curly, his is lighter, thick, and the longish strands hang perfectly at the nape of his neck.

"How about lunch?" he asks.

It's tempting, really. If anyone can make me feel better, it's Adam, but I'm not sure I want to feel better yet.

Being single is a wonderful and liberating thing. "Single and ready to mingle." "I'm every woman." "Put your hands up." "Truth hurts". There are so many songs about it, I can't even list them all. But the thing about the single girl anthem... it's usually born out of a lot of tears from the last heartbreak.

The girl power and celebration of singledom only comes after you've cried your eyes out and burned every item that belonged to the last man who did you wrong.

I'm still somewhere between the two, but I catch Adam's drift—it's probably time to re-enter the land of the living.

I let out a cleansing sigh. "Tomorrow. Breakfast tomorrow, I promise. I need to help Ava get our room organized." I glance over to the boxes stacked on top of my desk that I still haven't unpacked.

Adam doesn't look convinced.

"I said I promise."

He holds his pinky out and I roll my eyes but link it with mine.

"I'll swing by on my way to the dining hall. You've got an eight o'clock, yeah?"

I nod and groan. I am so not a morning person. "Yeah, but you don't."

"Preseason workouts this week and next at six. I'll be heading over to eat around that time anyway."

"Six o'clock in the morning?"

"Yeah. In the morning." The deep chuckle that follows makes me smile. He stands and ruffles my already messy hair.

"Stop it." I swat at his hand. He knows I hate it when he treats me like I'm twelve. In his mind, a three-year age gap makes him *so* much wiser.

"Be ready at quarter `til," he says as he moves to the door. "I'd hate to have to bang on the door and wake up the entire hall."

"God, you're obnoxious," I say, but he's already gone.

I get up and shower, hoping it washes away some of the lingering sadness along with the cracker crumbs. Back in my room, I look around it with fresh eyes and cringe. Ava's side is organized and decorated with bright colors and then there's my side. Even I can admit it looks a little depressing. Okay, a lot. White concrete walls, gray bed frame, and desk. The only color is my pale-yellow comforter.

After I'm dressed, I finally unpack. I didn't bring a lot of personal items because so many of them reminded me of Bryan. I fill the closet with my clothes and shoes, organize all of my school stuff on the desk, and I tape up a few pictures of my family and friends from high school on the wall.

Standing back, I survey the results. It's a start, and I feel a little more ready to face the world tomorrow. I flip on the small bedside light and crawl under the covers to sleep. I pick up my phone out of habit. Nothing good ever happens from scrolling your phone after midnight.

All of my friends from high school are posting selfies and tours of their new college dorms. There's Bryan, handsome as ever, in blue and orange. The college campus is in the background and he's lined up beside a group of big guys I assume are other football players based on their size. They hold beers and smile looking at the camera. He's obviously having no problem enjoying college without me.

That same handsome face I've known my whole life. We

were neighbors, childhood friends, and then high school sweethearts. I close my eyes and the last conversation I had with him replays in my mind.

"I don't understand. What do you mean you're not going to Valley? We're supposed to leave in three days." We lie on my bed and I'm still in that post-sex high, so it takes me a few seconds to realize he's serious.

His heavy weight on top of me suddenly feels claustrophobic. "I got a call from the coach at Boise State. One of their incoming freshmen got into a car accident. He's out all year, maybe longer."

"But we've been planning on going to college together for two years, and Idaho is like... a long way from Arizona. How is this going to work?"

He hesitates and runs a hand over his jaw while he studies me with an embarrassed look on his face.

"Oh my god. You're not just telling me you're going to Boise; you're ending this?" I motion between us.

"I don't think it would be fair to either of us to go to college with unrealistic expectations. You said it yourself, Idaho is a long way from Arizona. When we come back for holidays or summer vacations, we can pick up where we left off. You'll always be my perfect girl, Ginny." His gaze drops from my face to my cleavage and continues doing a long sweep of my naked body. The least a guy can do is avoid staring at your boobs while he breaks up with you. Or pull out. "But, I think we should give ourselves the freedom to explore and have fun while we're apart."

"Why would you break up with the perfect girl? That doesn't make any sense," I mutter quietly to the room, swiping a rogue tear. I didn't give him the satisfaction of seeing me cry then and I'm not going to let him ruin my first day of college tomorrow.

I force a smile as I reimagine all the amazing things college will bring without Bryan. For starters, I don't have to do anything I don't want to. I can be absolutely selfish with my time. Truthfully, I have no idea what that looks like anymore, but I'm ready to find out.

I put in my earbuds, hit play, and fall asleep with Beyoncé on repeat.

The next morning, Ava and I get ready for classes. She's got the TV hooked up and *Vampire Diaries* season one, episode one playing. Feels right somehow. The first season of everything starting today.

Our room finally looks like two excited freshmen live here. Ava's side is a little more personalized, photos of her and Trent, her boyfriend, take up most of the wall above her bed.

My roommate is in a serious relationship with her high school boyfriend, who is going to college upstate. It was something else we'd shared when we first connected over the summer, being in serious relationships. They don't seem concerned about the distance, although it's not nearly as far as Idaho.

Ava's been on the phone or texting him the better part of the last week since we moved in. She's nice and I think we'll be great roommates. I guess since she's in a relationship, at least I won't have to worry about her bringing random guys back to the dorm. Because I'll be starting college single and not exactly thrilled about the opposite sex, it'll be nice not to worry about that.

"Do you want to come to breakfast with us?" I ask as I'm preparing to leave.

"No thanks." She shakes her head, making her short, black

hair toss around her heart-shaped face. "I'm going to video chat with Trent on our way to our first classes."

A little pang of jealousy hits me, but I push it aside and head downstairs to meet Adam. Excited energy floats in the air. Blue and yellow banners hang on the front of the dorms welcoming us to the new school year.

Students are already out in droves heading off to classes, backpacks strapped to their shoulders, coffees in hand. They walk mostly in groups to their destinations; those who don't have earbuds in or stare down at their phones.

The Valley campus is truly beautiful. When we dropped Adam off before his freshman year and I got a look at the campus for the first time, I knew that it's where I wanted to go to college too. The buildings are mostly old and historic looking, green grass makes it feel a little less like the desert, and there's a huge fountain in the middle of campus.

"Ginny," Adam calls out, catching me by surprise while I'm lost people watching.

"Hey." I turn to see him and his friend and teammate Rhett with him.

"You remember Rauthruss?" Adam asks and runs a hand through his still-damp hair. Even wet it looks better than mine.

Rhett grins and steps forward with his hands shoved in his pockets. "Hey, Ginny. Good to see you again. Welcome to Valley."

Rhett Rauthruss is a giant man-boy. He's tall and built. His legs are like tree trunks. Seriously, his thighs could crush my head. But he's got this baby face and pouty mouth that keeps him from looking too intimidating. He's also got a really great Minnesota accent that I absolutely love.

He and Adam have been teammates and roommates since

their freshmen year, so I've met him a few times over the years and he came home with Adam once last semester for a weekend.

"Hey, Rhett, good to see you too."

He grins a little shyly.

"Are we ready?" Adam asks. "I'm starving."

My dorm doesn't have its own dining hall, so we cross the street to Freddy Dorm to eat. I follow Adam and Rhett inside, and we fall into the long line of people entering the dining hall, scanning their student ID cards as they go.

The smell of burned toast hangs in the air as we shuffle inside the busy dining room. Rhett heads off at a near jog for food, but Adam hangs back with me. "Grab food and then meet us at the big table in the right corner. You can't miss us."

With that, he rushes off too.

I do a lap while I check out the food options. Five or six different stations are set up with varying breakfast foods ranging from yogurt to omelets and everything in between.

I decide on waffles, get at the end of the line, and pick up a tray. The guy in front of me drums his fingers on the back of his tray impatiently. His fingers are long and strong-looking... somehow just really attractive. I let my gaze move up to his forearms and appreciate them in the same way. Tan and toned. The gray T-shirt he's wearing hugs his back and the short sleeves are snug against his biceps. Muscular but not too beefy.

When it's finally his turn, he sets the tray down and grabs a plate. With his profile to me, I take in his straight nose and sharp cheekbones. Dark, messy hair that I have the ridiculous urge to run my fingers through, sticks up on his head.

I think maybe I spent too many days in my dorm room crying over Bryan. I'm flat out gawking at this point, but it's a little hard not to. This guy is attractive without even getting a front view. He has this whole look about him that feels like he didn't bother glancing in the mirror this morning. Actually now that I think about it, it's a little frustrating that I spent twenty minutes taming my hair while he rolled out of bed and managed to look like that.

Damn. Welcome to Valley, Ginny.

He proceeds to fill his plate with four waffles. These aren't the size of the small, frozen waffles that you pop in the toaster, they are huge, bigger than my head waffles. He grabs a second plate and fills that one with bacon and eggs farther down the line. He glances between his plates and the food still left on the warmers ahead like he might not be finished.

I chuckle and he glances back at me. My breath hitches when his blue eyes meet mine. Not blue, a thousand shades of blue. He gives me a sheepish smile.

"Can you hand me another plate?" His deep voice washes over me, vibrating my insides. He's a lot to take in, but I do, not able to stop myself. His hair isn't only dark brown, it has hints of lighter strands too. It's like no part of him could decide on being one thing and instead he's made up of varying shades and depths.

He has an athletic build, tall but not towering over me like Bryan did. My ex was six foot four, which made him a great height to see over a mass of bodies on the football field, but not so great for kissing without standing on my tiptoes. I'm standing here wondering if I could kiss this guy flat-footed.

Aaand he asked me a question.

"Are you serious?"

He doesn't bat an eye, so I grab another plate and hand it to him.

"Thanks."

I fill my plate with one waffle like a reasonable human and

continue to scoot down the line behind him. He's added four
pieces of toast and a handful of grape jelly packets to the third
plate, and he's *still* eyeing the food ahead of us.

"Are you feeding a family of bears?"

One side of his mouth pulls up. "Just one very hungry
dude."

We reach the end of the line and he slows like he's waiting
for me. He eyes my tray. "Barely four hundred calories on that
plate. How are you going to make it to lunch?"

"Somehow I think I'll manage."

We start walking, both in the same direction.

"Are you following me?" I ask when we've walked shoulder
to shoulder for three steps.

"No. I think you're following me." We reach the table
where Adam and Rhett are seated with a group of guys.

"Yo, Heath!" one of the guys calls to him.

It takes a couple of seconds for my brain to catch up.

"You're a hockey player?" I frown while I try to place him.
I've only met a few of Adam's teammates, but I've been to
several games, so I'm surprised I don't recognize him.

His brows pull together studying me, maybe trying to place
me as well. "Not a fan of hockey? I think you're at the wrong
table then."

Adam stands and puts a protective arm around my shoulders. "She's not a fan of any men at the moment."

Kill me now.

I stare down at my white tennis shoes as Adam introduces
me. "Guys, this is my baby sister, Ginny. It's her first day."

The group offers their hellos and grunts of acknowledgment. They've all got several plates of food in front of them
like Heath and are shoveling it in like they haven't eaten in
days.

I take a seat and so does Heath, across from me.

"Did you come to the games last year?" he asks as he pours syrup over his waffles.

"Yeah, a couple. Why?"

"I don't recall seeing you."

This makes me laugh. In a crowd of cheering fans, how could he possibly remember? "I don't recall seeing you either."

He leans across the table with a cocky smirk. "I was the one doing all the scoring."

Continue reading Heath and Ginny's story in Secret Puck.

ACKNOWLEDGMENTS

Thanks so much to everyone who has continued this journey with me. Last year I thought I was ready to say goodbye to the smart jocks, but Sydney and Shaw's story wouldn't leave me alone until I wrote it! I hope you enjoyed going back to Valley and meeting some new characters, too. Will there be more? I'm not sure!

Thanks to my beta readers Amber, Amy, Anelise, and Katie. I adore you girls.

Thanks to Christine for keeping me organized, Jena for all the amazing graphic work, and Ellie for editing.

Made in the USA
Monee, IL
14 August 2022

11651020R00144